Praise for The Beast of Benfro

"Absolutely brilliant! I lost sleep rea not put it down. Meh sleep is over

"I was hooked from the and the ending is impressive to s.

"Suspenseful. Characters ... to root for..."

"I do enjoy a well written book..."

"Of all the Bigfoot books I've read, I've never seen where the author took this before. I'm off to read the sequel right now!"

"Great story and well put together - I will certainly read the sequel"

"Great book, keeps you guessing and the pages turning"

"Awesome page turner..."

Look out for the link at the back of this book for another monster tale absolutely free

Golden Hill Publishing
Golden Hill House
Pembroke
SA71 4SZ

Contents

The Beast
of
Benfro

Prologue

The break of early dawn offered the only illumination as the bone china cup was placed on its usual tray. Why was making the morning tea always his job, Beau wondered as he waited for water in the kettle to stop bubbling?

'You have to get up anyway to take your angina pills,' Judy had defended on the one occasion he'd voiced his disquiet. Today he sufficed with muttering how unfair it was that he never got to stay in bed. It might be true, but surely she could empty a couple of pills into a beaker and fetch a glass of water occasionally? Maybe after two heart attacks a bloody lie-in might be just the medicine he needed. Wasn't it the third that killed you?

Awakening the resentment fossilised over fifty years of marriage, Beau tipped the boiling water with too much acid verve, splashing a scolding punishment on his bare legs protruding from his too short, washed-up dressing gown (or housecoat as he insisted on calling it.)

"Damn!" he cried adding a few expletives under his breath as he shuffled to the sink to dab at the burn with a cold wet tea-towel. Still cursing Judy—this burn was her fault—he stopped dead, mid-dab, to stare through the window.

"What the…"

Dropping the towel, he hurried to the back door, its larger pane affording a better view of the garden. Heart pounding, Beau rotated the key, wincing that the click might scare it away as the latch drew back, despite his careful turning.

The creature remained, large as life at the bottom of his long garden. It definitely wasn't a dog, but it was far too big to be a cat. It was, wasn't it? A bloody panther in his garden. Bloody Hell's bells!

Turning the handle with equal care and equal volume to the clicking latch, the squeaking seemed never-ending as Beau tried desperately to be stealthy.

Whatever brought the panther onto his land had its full attention. Beau's wide eyes took it all in. A rush of fear bubbled through him; at what? Was he worried he would scare it away? Shaking his head, a wry smile played on his lips, dry with incredulity that he was able to stand with the door wide open without it caring.

Glancing around the shelves of his kitchen, he cursed Judy. "Where's that stupid cow put my camera? Why can't she ever leave anything in one sodding place?" he hissed. Camera-less, he stepped gingerly onto the slabs outside. Look at that! I'll never get this chance again!

Oblivious to his presence, Beau watched, eyes wide in the half-light as the big black cat slunk forward. "Oh my god! He's gonna pounce!" Beau bobbed on his toes barely containing a scream of glee.

As the beast pawed ahead, Beau strained from his place by the house unwilling to risk scaring away this marvel with a foot on the gravel. "Fuck it," he sighed. "I'll miss it if I don't move." As his slipper crunched, the beast flew forward. What was his prey? A rabbit?

The big cat was almost out of sight so Beau scurried across the gravel to keep it in view as long as possible. If that bitch hadn't hidden his camera...

His sudden scream was involuntary.

"Oh my god! Oh my god, no!" he cried, scurrying away from that which now filled his disbelieving view.

Beau scuttled backwards across the drive, never letting it out of his sight for a second.

Back to the house.

Back to safety.

Stumbling over his slippered feet, he had to get indoors, he had to. Thump-thump-thump his heart fought him to reach the house first, but in its rush it would stop them both.

Thump. Thump. Thuuummmp.

Beau clutched his chest. The pain shot down his arm as he fell to one knee. His gargoyle face stared in disbelief as the creature thudded towards him. It must have followed the panther... He should have stayed inside.

That was the last thought Beau ever had.

With a final grimace, he collapsed in a convulsing heap mere feet from his kitchen door until his limp body lay still and unresponsive—even to the mighty poke it received from the monstrous, hair-covered finger as it thrust into his chest again and again.

Chapter One

"James! Wake up!" he cried with a palm over his mouth, kicking out at his brother's ankle as it dangled off the sofa from under the dog blanket. With a frown, David glanced across at the blanket-less dog bed and shook his head. "Get up, now. I don't want Marcus to see you like this!"

"Like what, Dad?"

It was too late. His brother's embarrassing antics would surely get back to his wife now.

"Nothing, Marcus. Uncle Jimmy's not feeling too well, that's all," David soothed. "Go and get yourself a pop-tart or something, okay?"

Watching Marcus disappear, he was grateful Sara's college was still on half-term for a few more days guaranteeing she wouldn't rise from bed until this afternoon.

Yanking the dog blanket away, David threw it back to its rightful place in Jess's basket then hauled Jimmy to an upright position and slapped his face; gently at first, but when gentle didn't work, he happily increased the ferocity.

"Hey, gerroff!" Jimmy's first words spewed forth.

"Oh good. It lives," David sneered. "Now get up and clear this mess up."

Jimmy bolted with sudden speed towards the toilet. "Sorry…" he gargled before the unmistakeable sound of vomiting filled the air.

"Close the door!" David barked as he collected the cans and… what was that… No! David sank on the couch and sniffed the rolled up dog-end to confirm what he already knew. How had Jimmy managed to find marijuana in this sleepy village?

He still sat with it pinched between thumb and forefinger when Marcus returned with a pop-tart bitten into the shape of an aeroplane which he was whooshing through the sky.

"Can't you just eat that normally? Come on. You're making crumbs. What would Mum say?"

"She lets me," Marcus insisted, bringing the plane to a crash landing on the coffee table as his gun turret mouth 'shot' a wing. Scooping the debris into his mouth, more crumbs tumbled to the floor and down his school shirt.

"Marcus!" David seethed. "Go and brush your teeth. We'll be late!"

Marcus skipped off, his father's anger meaning nothing to him. He knew who ruled this house, and just because she was away didn't mean he was about to abide the laws of this temporary regime.

Staggering from the downstairs toilet, Jimmy mouthed 'Sorry' over and over with placatory palms held up.

Slumping back onto the sofa, he fumbled around for the blanket, and when he couldn't find it, he hugged a cushion to him. Pointing the TV remote at the screen which dominated half the room, Jimmy stabbed at the uncooperative buttons, his hand trembling, a shiver made him judder.

"It's not even cold, Jimmy. It's that stuff," David gestured to the mess of tobacco and papers and beer cans at his brother's feet. "That's what's making you feel like this." He shook his head. "Where did you even find this?" he placed the stubby joint on the table in front of Jimmy.

"Oh, thanks, man! I thought I'd lost it!"

"Don't! Don't smoke it in here. Monique will go ballistic!"

"Yeah, well, she's five thousand miles away, isn't she."

"Four and a half…" David shook and frowned. "But that isn't the point. She wouldn't put up with you behaving this way, and I'm not happy about it either."

Stomping from the room in a show of strength, he turned and addressed his brother once more. "I'm taking Marcus to school. Clear this up before I get back… I'm Skyping Monique and…" he glanced around the room and sighed. "Just clear it up!"

Jimmy raised a hand. "Will do, boss," he nodded before sliding back to lying down and cranking the volume up on the crappy documentary which had dubious experts alluding to the confirmed existence of mermaids. He was snoring before David reached the stairs. "Marcus! Come ON! We're late."

Marcus appeared at once, back-pack slung over one shoulder which he rounded to keep in place. Shooting David an acid look of indignation, he flopped down the stairs in an insolent rhythm of contempt.

"Ready?" David ventured, and Marcus nodded.

As his son skipped to their car in the driveway, David barked his orders to Jimmy once more. When he closed the door and turned, he forced a smile on his face and muttered under his breath at the sight of the elderly man in his driveway.

"Ah, hello 'H'" His name was Hywel, but on David's constant mispronunciation, they'd settled on an amusing 'H' instead. "I'm in a bit of a hurry," he warned. "Gotta get Marcus off to school." He rolled his eyes as if it was a burden they both shared, but it was unlikely H had ever taken his son to school as the old Victorian building he would have attended was visible from here anyway.

"Sorry, David. It won't take a minute."

No, I bloody know it won't. It'll take twenty at least.

With a resolved sigh and a growled order to Marcus to get in the car (which he ignored and proceeded to kick a football around in the road), David prepared to listen to his neighbour's urgent ordeal.

"It's about your son... Marcus..." he added for unnecessary clarity. "I don't mind him playing on my field, but not the ones at the top."

"Oh, okay. You hear that, Marcus? Stay away from Mr Jones' top fields." Marcus gave no indication he'd listened and ran around in a slow-motion victory dance at the goal he'd just scored into next-door's drive. "Marcus!"

"There are abandoned mines up there. I don't need to tell you how dangerous they are…"

No, but you will if I don't make a sharp exit. Backing away and opening the car door, David smiled and nodded. "No, of course." He paused from stepping in as H continued.

"How's your wife? Lovely woman. Very pretty."

Thanks, H. I hadn't noticed.

"Away, isn't she?"

You know she is, David grew his smile to hide his irritation.

"Any good pictures, yet? Found any new species?"

"I don't know, H. I haven't spoken to her yet. I'm Skyping her when I get back." If I ever leave.

Hywel frowned.

"Skype? It's a video call thing. On my computer…"

H nodded enthusiastically. "Say 'bore da' from me won't you?"

"Yes, yes. Of course." Now go away, please!

"I used to be a bit of a primatologist, myself. Well biologist really. I just love it all, I do."

Fascinating, David seethed. "You'll have to tell me about it another time. That would be great," he lied.

"Who was that chap? The one she went off with?" H chuckled, "I wouldn't let my pretty wife go on a trip with him, I don't mind telling you. Ruggedly handsome. You know the fella?"

"Mm Hm," David winced. "That's 'Brad.' He's the survival expert and guide through the Congo, I think," David bristled —*and* one time lover of my wife whom she didn't mention would be on this expedition. Fabulous.

"Very cosy they were…" H prepared to launch into more, but David cut him off with another yell at his son to get in the car.

"Sorry," he said, despite the temptation to torture himself with more regaling of his wife's duplicity, he didn't have time. "We have to go," and he slammed his door before H could utter another word. Looking backwards to reverse from the drive, he didn't even glance back at the house before zooming from their little cul-de-sac.

"We're collecting Daryn," Marcus announced just after David had turned the car in the other direction.

"You could have said!" he snapped

Marcus shrugged and slouched in the passenger seat, feet resting on the dashboard. "Just did."

David sighed and pulled a U-turn. "We're going to be late, you know that, don't you…"

Marcus shrugged again.

16

Chapter Two

David offered a skyward look of thanks as the aging Volvo of another neighbour he'd rather avoid stood idle in its drive, the house beyond dark and still. More forced friendliness would have sealed the deal on their tardiness, although the undeniable allure of Mari Mathias would have made for an altogether more palatable distraction. But, this morning, she had yet to wake her leisurely self and David was grateful.

When they reached Daryn's, he wasn't waiting outside his house in spite of the lateness and dry weather. Marcus oozed out of the car as only a prepubescent can; more because he'd prefer to share the back seat with his friend than travel up front with his father (having already established its control—his big sister being absent.)

There was a long wait while Daryn gathered his school bag and put his shoes on. David clenched his fists against the steering wheel. He couldn't miss the video call with Monique. Goodness knows when she'd be somewhere with signal again.

"Come on!" he growled unheard from inside the car. When Daryn sauntered to the window and offered a smiling thank you for the lift, David's grip on the wheel eased. How polite. It was more than he'd received from anyone in his household for a while. "You're welcome, Daryn."

Glancing from one boy to the other, he hoped the message of gratitude at the politeness was being absorbed by his son. He doubted it.

As they travelled to the bus stop, the boys sat in silence apart from nudging each other and sniggering. David pushed aside the fact it might be about him. Why would it? Reaching across, he turned on the radio.

"...The Beast of Benfro... We've had a huge response to this... mainly that I'm wrong," chuckled the excruciatingly jolly voice of the morning DJ. It grated on David but he couldn't be bothered to find another station.

"Apparently, I shouldn't mix Welsh with English! According to a text I'm reading, I should say 'Yr Bwystfil o Benfro', which is a mouthful, you have to agree! And that's still wrong 'cos that just means Pembroke, not Pembrokeshire... That's from a Llewellyn Jenkins. Thanks for that, I think... He goes on to suggest 'The Beast of Pembrokeshire.' Not as catchy in my opinion!"

"My dad's seen it," Daryn spoke for the first time since entering the car. "Well, he's seen what it's done."

"Your dad?" David scowled in the rear-view mirror.

Marcus rolled his eyes. They were getting a great workout recently. "Daryn doesn't live with his dad... He's got a farm up in the mountains."

David nodded and raised his eyebrows in invitation for Daryn to continue.

"Makes a hell of a mess of the sheep. And the cows. He's got both, see." He shifted in his seat and his face reddened. "You won't believe it, but my dad says it's definitely something big."

"I do believe you, Daryn. Trust me."

Marcus rolled his eyes again in anticipation of David's favourite story.

"A panther's not that far-fetched. They can travel an easy forty or fifty miles a day, and there's sightings of them all over the place—probably the same one." He coughed, ready to recount his tale. "I was walking Jess in the woods up on Preseli Top…"

"Foel Cwmcerwyn?" Daryn queried.

David frowned and shrugged. "What's that?"

"Foel Cwmcerwyn. It's the top of the mountain. 'Bare hill of the white rock valley,' or something," Daryn advised.

"Probably… anyway… I was walking through the woods up there when Jess went weird; growling, hackles up. As I reached her, there was the unmistakable sound of a big cat. Not a roar… a kind of 'raww rawww.' You'd know it if you heard it… Unmistakable," he repeated.

David reddened at the next part. "I didn't see it, but when I exited the trees, there was a family; a man, a woman, and a teenage girl, striding towards me. I should have warned them, but I felt foolish. I'd only walked

19

about half a mile when a terrible scream echoed through the pass." David coughed again.

"Rushing back, I saw them running from the woods. Nothing was chasing them and they seemed fine, but I've always felt a bit guilty. What if something had happened?" David always paused at this juncture to allow his audience to pardon him; to say, 'I'd have done the same;' and, 'they probably wouldn't have believed you anyway.' He was disappointed but not surprised when Daryn said nothing.

As they approached the bus stop, the bus was already pulling out. If they didn't get on it, David would have to drive them all the way to town. He'd definitely miss his call with Monique then, and that was unthinkable. He had some questions for his wife.

Flooring the accelerator, David pulled out into oncoming traffic, cars swerving to avoid him. Horn slammed and lights flashing, he edged in front of the departing bus. With a glance in his side mirror, he yanked hard on the steering wheel and braked, forcing ten tonnes of metal and flesh to an uncomfortable brake-squealing halt.

As the dust fell, David waved an apology to appease the scowling driver. He kept the smile etched on his face as the two boys shuffled at an unrushed pace to the door and climbed aboard. Thank goodness.

The red clock on the dash glowered the time at him, eight forty-five. He'd be home in time. Monique wasn't calling until nine.

Pulling back into the morning traffic with a gentle waft of the pedal, he scooted along the by-pass in its steep sided wooded gorge and breathed a deep sigh as he reached the leafy rural idyll of Pleasant Valley.

"... A suggestion has come in for 'The Pembrokeshire Panther.' What do we think? I like it," The DJ persisted. *"But I still prefer my original title. 'The Beast of Benfro.' Being Welsh* and *English, represents our fine county, don't you agree? We all speak a bit of Welsh, don't we? And 'beast' rather than panther, because what if it's not a panther? Hey? Some texts have come in suggesting it might be something even bigger. Give us your thoughts..."*

David didn't listen to how he could get in touch with the bubbly man because he was back in his drive and had turned the radio off. His hurrying hand shot for the handle but stalled at opening the car door. Reluctant for the inevitable sleeping slob on his couch, and the untidy mess he was sure would still be there, he was also hesitant to hear Monique's excuses for why she hadn't told him about Brad.

Biting his lip, he pushed it open and dawdled into the house examining a rose petal that had withered around the edge. It felt like a metaphor, but he didn't want to think about for what. Himself, probably.

Once inside, he threw the front door shut, hoping the slam might wake his unwelcome houseguest. As the reverberation died down, David's heart thumped in his throat at voices from the lounge: Jimmy's, and the unmistakeable smooth Frenchness of his wife's. Scurrying down the hall, he barged in, ashen faced. "Monique!"

Drooped on the couch, Jimmy was in bleary-eyed banter, via the airwaves, with his sister-in-law; her tanned face, blending with a dusty backdrop of an African settlement somewhere, was balanced precariously on coffee table debris. David ushered his brother away with violently flapping arms and perched in his place on the sofa, an apologetic grin attempting to conceal what his eyes failed to hide. Damn. This wasn't supposed to have happened.

"Monique, darling. You've phoned early."

Her sunburned forehead creased as she answered, "Have I?" She looked at her watch. Eyebrows arching in recognition of her time zone miscalculation, she sneered, "Good job I did. How long has that fool been staying in my house?"

"Our house..." David mumbled.

"I can see the state of the place, David. Get him to tidy his mess, and get him out. I don't want him near my children, do you hear me? He's a bad influence."

"He's fine," David winced, vowing to make Jimmy pay for this. What on earth was he doing answering his video call and putting him in this position?

"He's not fine. I can see beer cans everywhere. For god's sake, David! Is he using? Tell me he's not using in my house!"

David shook his head and widened his grin. "No, of course not," his paleness was almost blue now and he was in danger of fainting. Rousing himself, his heart pumped just enough blood through his veins to flush his cheeks scarlet as he remembered his own grievance. "Why didn't you mention Brad was going with you on this trip?"

Monique's scowl deepened. "Don't, David. Don't you dare try and divert from your delinquent brother. You *know* why I didn't tell you about Brad. I didn't want you to be uncomfortable... You know how you can get." Her French accent, muted by years in Essex had now taken an unwelcome Australian twang. He could thank Brad for that, he supposed.

David's cheeks burned. Wasn't his discomfort the exact reason she should have told him? The anger boiled but David didn't have the energy to show it. He opened his mouth to speak, but Monique shot him down.

"Do you trust me? You do trust me, don't you, David? Because if you don't..."

It was a phrase that didn't need finishing. She'd said it before and David didn't want to be reminded how it ended; 'I may as well do what I'm being accused of.' The words swirled in his head. Through gritted teeth, he reassured her that of course he trusted her, and that he was sorry for even mentioning it.

"Well, this has been nice," Monique's sarcasm was unmistakeable. With a long sigh she added, "I don't know when I'll be able to call again. We're going deep into the jungle."

"Any good pictures yet?" David desperately tried to keep her on the line, partly from missing her, but mainly not wanting to leave her alone again with Brad. "Of the Bili ape, or whatever?"

"Or whatever? You know it's a bloody Bili Ape. It's not a difficult name to remember, is it? Don't start being stupid." She elongated the last syllable. With a sudden turn, Monique allowed a smile of genuine warmth to pass through the laptop screen, the gap in her teeth drawing David's gaze. He missed that mouth.

"Look, I 'ave to go. We've got a long trek and we need to make it to camp before dark. Speak soon, okay?"

Her face went fuzzy and David missed the chance to say his goodbyes. It was just as well, his throat was too constricted to release his words anyway.

Chapter Three

"**W**hy?"

Jimmy shrugged. "I didn't think you'd want to miss her. I'm right, aren't I?"

It was impossible to remain angry in the face of such logic. David nodded. "I just wish it was a bit tidier."

In the spirit of gratitude, Jimmy bent down and picked up an empty beer can. Standing with it in his hand, he looked to relieve himself of it. Floundering, with red cheeks he balanced it with the tobacco, cold cups of tea and snack remains littering the coffee table.

Wide eyes met his brother's, searching approval he knew wouldn't be there. They held one another's gaze for a moment until David broke the silence with a raucous guffaw. "You are a useless tool, James Webb!"

Jimmy joined in the laughter just in time before the soberness of the situation brought David to sudden silence. With stern severity, he turned to Jimmy. "Clean this mess up. Bin bags are in the kitchen. I'm going to walk Jess."

He knew where she'd be. Taking the stairs two at a time, he paused outside Sara's room. Knocking once, then again, louder. He was sure there came a grunt from inside. Turning the handle, he pushed open the door slowly in case permission hadn't been granted and he could rapidly close it again if "Get out, Dad," was screamed at him.

Peeping in, Jess lay curled on Sara's blanketed feet. "Jess. Jesss!" he hissed.

Sara grunted and glared out from under the covers.

"Just taking Jess for a walk, sweetie. Sorry."

Sara hauled the covers over her head, grumbling as Jess took her sweet time.

David smiled to witness Jimmy unravelling the roll of bin bags as he passed the lounge. "See you later," he called as he closed the front door.

Jess hovered at the back of the car making feeble leaps. "Come here, you." David grabbed her and placed her in the hatch-back of the VW.

A short drive of a mere half a mile brought him to the dramatic Colby woods. David pulled into the swish new car-park. There had been a lot of work building walls and felling trees of late. Whole swathes of forest had disappeared in the Forestry Commission's harvest of their plantation from thirty years ago. Hills, which had been covered in forest when they'd moved here, now baulked at their baldness, although, nature's rapid recovery in providing new shrubs and greenery was more than impressive.

Jess found the hop from the boot easier than the jump in. She scampered into the woods, choosing one of several paths. "Okay, we'll take that one," David winced before prizing a smile onto his lips in despair at his sadness that even Jess took him for granted. "You stupid sod," he berated with an incredulous shake of his head. "Call her back if you want to go somewhere different!"

He didn't. Jess took this path through being in tune with her master, he realised. It was the route he would have chosen anyway, she didn't have a preference. As he watched her sniff and squat at every scent to leave her own, her sheer exuberance calmed him. "Good girl, Jess," he said. She looked back at him and wagged. 'I know,' she said.

The further they walked into the woods, the further away his troubles seemed. Jess ran ahead, but never so far as to be a worry, and when she returned, the love in her spaniel eyes clutched his heart in their brown pools.

David patted her soft old head and she scampered away, and David felt the warmth of pride at her incredible sprightliness for her thirteen years. It was a beautiful morning. Jess had chosen her pathway well. From here, he could link up to another trail that crossed the stream at the bottom of the valley. A hike to the top of the mountain-like hill on the other side would carry on all the way to the beach at Amroth.

An ice-cream and a beer whilst gazing upon the azure ocean wouldn't harm his improving mood; unless the stillness gave him too much time to think.

Images of Monique and Brad assaulted his thoughts once more. So far away from him. So close to Brad. Such an intimate space. Could she really resist his undeniable charm? David wasn't sure he would in her shoes.

Then, thinking of temptation bolstered him. He had resisted his own when it had come calling not so long ago, although, temptation was perhaps too strong a word. The mature enticements of Mari Mathias could never compete with Monique's youthful ardour. But it had been flattering, especially after learning of Monique's past with Brad. A past she had kept from him until chancing upon some old photos had forced her to tell.

His smile grew lopsided as he wrestled with discomfort at his insecurities. The image of Mari stroking his thigh when he'd accepted a lift back from the beach after another beery morning stroll almost made him laugh out loud. It was Jess's fault. She loved Mari's two Lurchers, although she could never get near them, they were so fast.

He'd sat in her ancient red Volvo wondering why she didn't set off immediately. At first, the conversation seemed to be about dogs: how it was surprising how well Jess, being so much older, still got on well with her young pups; how they could offer a lot to one another. She'd rubbed his leg for quite a while before his beer-soaked brain caught her meaning. She brushed it all off as a big joke when David said he'd never be unfaithful to his wife.

"No, no of course. Of course," she'd said. "But if you ever need to talk, or anything..."

David had demonstrated gratitude, and he'd felt it too. Mari was a very attractive lady. She'd make a toy boy very happy!

He was jolted from his gentle musings by a terrifying growl from Jess. Ten metres in front, she stared out across the valley, hunched down, fur standing on end. He didn't know how he could tell; what subtle element of her body language gave the clue, but he knew she was scared.

"Jess! What is it, girl?"

She stayed put, but edged back along the path. She hadn't behaved like this since the panther in the Preseli's. Maybe that would be a good name to suggest to the Radio DJ—Preseli Panther? He couldn't believe he'd been distracted and forced his attention back to his troubled dog.

"Jess. Come here. Come on, girl!"

Jess didn't come. Instead, she showed uncharacteristic disobedience and stayed steadfastly growling at the trees.

What if it was the panther again? She could be in danger. David didn't remember the recommended procedure to avoid mutilation from a big cat. Acting on his instinct to run to Jess making as much noise as possible, with heart thumping, he raced to her yelling her

29

name, his thudding feet echoing from the steep valley walls.

A piercing screech at once terrified and comforted him as his mind struggled to recognise what it was. The cogs whirred and fell into place. Peacocks! It was a screech like a peacock. There were a pair in the woods in Pleasant Valley and he heard them frequently; not usually this time of day, but later at dusk. If they were away from their home for some reason and had spotted Jess through the trees, of course they'd cry out, wouldn't they?

Reaching her, he snorted air into his hungry lungs, his chest cramping as she failed to calm in his presence. Hairs on the back of his neck sent a shudder down his spine as the terror in her eyes reached his.

"What is it, girl? Hey?" He looked along the trajectory of her gaze. Peacocks could be frightening to an old dog, he supposed. Especially displaying their bright tail feathers.

As he stared across the valley, his eyes didn't pick out the bright blue and green crescent he expected. What they did fall on creased his face in a frown of confusion. What was that?

Squinting in disbelief, he shook his head. Jess growled furiously. A man in a costume, surely. A big man.

With a sigh, David knew at once the explanation. Pembrokeshire had become quite the Hollywood film set lately. Harry Potter, Robin Hood, Snow White and The Huntsman, to name but three, all shot scenes locally. A

Bigfoot film must be in the making. They'd have to add the soundtrack later, or pay Jess royalties. Suspecting he was fooling himself, he laughed nervously.

"It's okay, Jess. It's just a film, see?" Craning his neck, a vein throbbed in his throat as his heart pounded in his chest. "Come on, Jess. It's just a film," his voice a whine now as he tripped backwards in scurrying footsteps

But it wasn't, he knew it wasn't, and any doubts David's pragmatism had attempted to put in his way crumbled in the face of what he saw now.

Across the cwm, half a mile away as the crow flies, a beast sniffed the air eight foot off the ground as it stood proud and glared at him. As their eyes met, David flinched as the coldness of the predator forced his gaze away. There was no possibility it could be a suited actor.

With a screech, the creature lunged.

David's legs scrambled beneath, but failed to move him forward, forcing his bulging eyes to watch with growing terror as the creature hurtled towards him. Trees splitting in each mighty stride, its bulk ploughed through them like meadow hay.

The distance seemed far, but not far enough as the powerful beast ran down the hillside at an impossible swiftness. Dark hair covering its entire body ruffled in the wind as it tore, grunting with each foot thud on the ground, down the slope.

"Jess!" he cried. "We have to go. Now!" Wrenching his gaze away, his legs wobbled and he stumbled over his feet. "Come ON, Jess!" he screamed again, but Jess was already running. Much as she wanted to protect her master from whatever it was, running away was the best plan. With glances back to say, 'See? I told you,' she kept herself firmly at David's feet.

Their morning stroll had been brief, but now, in their terror, the car seemed so far away.

Branches cracked in their ears. They'd never out run this monster.

Rounding the corner, David skidded to a halt and gasped. Mari's Volvo estate sat parked impossibly close to his car. Flinching in panic, he knew she must have planned to keep him there until she returned. But, where was she? Hopefully, a long way down a different path.

Squeezing between the two cars, David fumbled in his pocket for his keys. "Come on!" he coached. His finger finally finding the button on the key fob. The lights blinked and the handle opened. "Damn!" he hissed as his door clanged into Mari's.

Wriggling, he still couldn't force his body through the gap. Certain the creature would fly around the corner any second, he had to find a way in.

Dashing to the back of his car flung him backwards as his coat sleeve snagged on the Volvo door handle. Frantic, he tugged. Not budging, he jerked it wildly back and forth until it ripped and he was finally free.

Flinging open the hatch-back, he heaved Jess's bulk into the boot space and dived in after her. Reaching his trembling arm up he yanked at the strap and tugged the boot shut.

Scrambling over the back row, he fought into the driver's seat and thrust the key into the ignition. The car roared into life and David threw it in reverse. The wheels spun, showering stones everywhere as he shot back, crunched into first gear, and raced from the car-park.

Beads of sweat trickled down his forehead as the relief of escape finally slowed his heart rate. But with a look back came a wave of guilt that made him gag. What about Mari?

Chapter Four

What should he do? He had no idea which path Mari might have taken, only that she wasn't on the same one as him or he would have run into her as he fled. Should he call her name? No. It might bring her into danger rather than away from it.

Absently, he plucked his phone from his pocket, but there was no signal in the dense woodland. Flooring the accelerator, David's wheels spun as he flew from the dark lane onto the country road that led back to Pleasant Valley and home.

Tyres screeched as he squealed around the corner into his little cul-de-sac, Pen Y Cwm (Head of the Valley), and up to his house at the top of the hill (which they had imaginatively named 'Valley View.')

Stones sprayed into the air as the VW screeched into the drive. The driver door flew open before the car had finished coming to an abrupt halt.

Fumbling keys into the lock, at last he made it inside. Running to the phone in the kitchen: the only one attached to the wall and guaranteed not to be out of charge, he unhooked the handset and dialled... 9... 9... 9.

"Police, please... and hurry!"

"Calm down, sir. What seems to be the trouble?"

'I'm worried my neighbour is being eaten by a sasquatch' sounded ridiculous, so he omitted that when he yelled, "My neighbour is being attacked. Colby woods. I'll meet you there…"

"No, stay on the line please, sir. Don't put yourself in unnecessary danger!"

But David had already gone. As he reversed at speed from the drive, he wondered for a brief moment where his brother was before pushing it from his mind. The lazy bastard was probably stoned again, but he didn't have time to ponder his failings now. That could wait.

Mari's car was still as he'd left it, so he waited nearby with the engine running ready to make a sharp getaway if needed.

Stretching towards the window, he couldn't see far into the woods, and he certainly couldn't see Mari.

Nausea overtook him. "Where are you?" he breathed, and a wave of sick reached his mouth. Gulping it down only added to the queasiness and he had to open the door for fresh air.

Bile burned his nose and stung the back of his eyes, but he managed to swallow just as the police Ford Fiesta pulled into the car-park and he managed an uneasy smile.

Coming to a stop behind him, two doors swung open and one male and one female police officer ran over to him. "Did you phone the police?" the stocky male asked.

David nodded. Should he tell them what he saw? He had little choice. It wasn't that long ago he'd almost cost a young family dearly when he'd cowardly not told them about the panther in the Preseli hills. So, he had to tell them all he knew. He couldn't cope with the guilt again.

Chapter Five

"**S**ome sort of creature... not a panther, but bigger... that's what you're telling me?"

"I know it sounds stupid. A man in a gorilla suit was my first thought... You know? With all the films they shoot around here."

The policeman looked unimpressed. "And that's what you want me to write in my report, is it?"

David nodded. "Well, it's the truth. What else would you write?"

The officer scribbled on his pad and read back the last few words. "*Not a man in a gorilla suit...* Thank you, sir. That will be all for now. We'll have a look for Mrs Mathias. We may need to speak to you again, so, don't leave town."

Shaking off the awful feeling he was under suspicion, because that was ridiculous, wasn't it? He said "Okay," and got back in his car.

The short drive back home took forever. Calmness at a buck passed combined with a frowning scrutiny of his thoughts as they bobbed and crashed in his head. What would the police find? Mari safe, or...? If that thing had got to her, what might have happened? No. She'd be fine.

She must have taken a different path or he'd have seen her.

It was with a mollified sigh that he pulled back into the drive, and the relief continued when he walked in to the sound of vacuuming.

Standing at the doorway, a smile crept on his face. It wasn't Sara, risen from her dark womb, but Jimmy looking all domesticated. Unseen, David couldn't resist. Stifling laughter, he crept forward and tapped his brother on his shoulder. The guffaws exploded unhindered at the death white of Jimmy's face as he clutched his chest with one hand and rested on the vacuum cleaner wand with the other...

Through gasps for breath, Jimmy laughed and shook his head. The humour was welcome and drew a line under this morning's anger.

Stopping short of hugging, they exchanged coy smiles ending in uncomfortable leg-tapping. "I'll be in my office if you need me," David said moving towards the door.

'Sorry' played on Jimmy's lips but fell back within the confines of his unexpressed intentions. When David was out of earshot, Jimmy kicked the switch on the cleaner and collapsed back on the sofa. The floor half vacuumed, he'd finish after a break. The job of crawling from the dog-house: complete.

Reaching forward, with a groan, he plucked the rolled up joint from the table and brought it to his lips. Pausing just before it reached them, he thought better of it and plopped it into his jacket pocket instead. Half-cleaning the room had tired him out. With a yawn, he closed his eyes and settled for a nap.

David sat at his computer in silence. The tranquil state he usually crunched through the figures was held out of reach by images of what he'd seen through the trees. It was when his legs hit the top of the foot well of his desk that he first noticed them shaking.

Tea slopped over his mouse mat, "Damn!" he hissed. Taking a deep breath, he placed his hands with care on the arms of his ergonomic masterpiece of an office chair, but they wouldn't stay still; the square face of his watch drummed against the chair frame.

Jolting from a tickling on his forehead, droplets of sweat sprayed onto the screen. Gingerly, he reached a palm to his head.

"Mari!" he cried. "Please be all right."

Picturing himself riding into the forest in a suit of armour, sword held high ready to slay the beast. Instead, he'd done his usual and run away. "You did everything you could," he assured himself. "Calling her might have brought her into danger," he addressed his blank monitor. The police are on the case now. They have the manpower to rescue her safely.

Another deep breath and he powered up the screen that had retreated to standby from inactivity. Numbers blurred into one-another. He couldn't work now. He was already behind, but he would be doing his client no favours if he insisted on working in this state.

Pushing his keyboard away, he planted his feet on the floorboards and sighed. What if they didn't find her? Or worse; they only found bits of her? Ripped limb from limb by an unknown monster?

Already the doubts had set in. It wasn't possible that he'd seen what he thought he'd seen. The woods weren't big enough to support such a large animal. And whilst a panther could travel fifty miles a day unseen, there was no way an eight foot yeti or sasquatch or whatever the fuck that was could do the same.

It had to be a man in a suit. He must have witnessed a carefully crafted film set. Trees falling away mechanically in some clever special effects sequence. The creature aided by ropes and wires to glide through the vegetation with such ease.

His mind clamped onto the explanation, but a jittery voice in the background refused to be silenced. He knew what he'd seen.

Still, he typed into the search bar of his computer 'Filming in Pembrokeshire.' All the familiar ones filled the screen. Famous faces 'Their Finest,' a film about Dunkirk starring the fabulous Bill Nighy and exquisite Gemma Arterton. David's cheeks flushed admitting a crush on the pretty actress and realising how close she'd been and he hadn't known about it until now.

Squashing the colour from his lips, musing on what it might have been like to chance a meeting with her drew guilt to flush his cheeks further. Brief guilt for Monique (but it was okay to fancy a film star, wasn't it? And a harmless crush couldn't compare to the duplicitous inclusion of an ex-lover on an overseas assignment; especially when she'd kept it from him), but more guilt for Mari.

The feelings of attraction stirred by Hollywood images reminded him that despite his rebuff, Mari's attention had been welcome. Pushing himself up, he walked over to the window and peered out. No sign of her car. But it had only been what, an hour?

He couldn't work. He couldn't go for a walk—he'd be terrified. But he needed to get away. Bolting from his office, the slouching figure of Sara gripping the bannister at the last few steps of the staircase.

"Morning, sweetie." Even a grunt was too much to expect. "Everything okay?"

Sara paused in her shuffling to glare at him. "It was until you woke me up!"

Fatherly criticism stalled at his lips and he settled for a weak smile and a "Sorry." Sure of the answer before he spoke, he asked anyway, "I'm going for a drive; change of scene. Fancy coming out with your old dad?"

A sneer creased Sara's face. 'Oh, please!' it exclaimed. 'I'd rather die.'

Hiding the hurt, David called out goodbye to anyone who cared and got behind the wheel as soon as he could. Pushing the button to start the engine, its unexciting warble sank his mood more. Why couldn't he be roaring off in something more exciting? Why was he so dull? No wonder Monique had fallen for Brad.

Spinning shingle behind him, he raced from the close and through the valley. At the end he steered south, the turquoise ocean glinting its calming light beckoned him forward. Gripping the steering wheel, willing the roof to fold back on his car, he knew he was skirting the fringe of a mid-life crisis.

Pulling the car onto the beach, he turned off the engine, yanked open the door and stood on the sand. Breathing the salty ozone air, desperate for peace to wash over him, but it didn't and tension gripped even harder. Forcing a smile to his lips, he took manic deep breaths but calmness refused. Flopping on the sand, he threw his head in his hand and sighed. When he brought his face up again, his eyes were red and dewy. Unsure exactly where his torment was from, he prayed to the crashing waves, "Let Mari be okay. Please."

Chapter Six

Tapping the steering wheel with fidgeting fingers, he swung the car dangerously around the constricted bends. Narrowly squeezing between a bush and a bus, David's heart raced as he pulled out into the centre of the road again.

Surging up the hill, the view of the valley opened out before him, but not a view of Mari's car. That was still conspicuous by its absence. Particularly as in its place was a blue and yellow Battenberg squad car.

"I take it they haven't found her then?" he said to himself. "They're not going to find her in there, are they?" Cruising past to his own house at the top of the hill, he passed 'H' leaning on a spade on one of the vacant plots. "Stay there, 'H,'" he muttered through the gritted teeth of a coerced smile. "I don't have time for another of your monologues."

Glancing over his shoulder at the police car, he shut the door firmly and leaned against it. With a sigh he called out "I'm back," to the expected indifference, and sure enough, an apathetic silence greeted his ears. He made it to his office, slid the lock on the door and sagged into his desk chair.

He prodded his stubbled chin with apexed index fingers, toying with firing up his desktop again. After conceding he'd never twist his mind back to work, he applied to take the day off, sanctioning himself immediately. Leaning back, he let out a sigh. The sighs soon turned to snores.

He woke the first time when he toppled from his finger perch. Adjusting the ergonomic chair, he was soon hiding from his troubles in unconscious anxiety. He would not be able to hide for long.

Chapter Seven

"**D**avid! David!! Wake the fuck up, will ya?" The chair almost tumbled back as Jimmy shook his brother awake. "Wha..? Who..?"

"Get up, David. It's the filth. They're at the door! And before you jump down my throat, it's you they want to see."

David was roused to full consciousness now. "Are you sure? You bloody stink of weed."

Jimmy shrank back into his shoulders like a coy turtle. Big brown eyes attempted a puppy-dog reverie. "I might've had a little puff of that joint you found me," – careful to include his brother in a share of the blame. "Tidying was stressful, man."

David fixed a look of contempt and glared at his little brother who towered above him despite his guilty hunched shoulders. "Well, what do they want?"

"Dunno. They asked to speak to you."

David's heart raced, pumping blood to his brain which swiftly came up with the answer. With a smile and a shake of his head, he assured Jimmy. "Don't worry. They've just come to keep me up to date about Mari." Jimmy frowned in non-comprehension and David's smile dropped. "I hope it's good news."

Heart pounding again, this time it couldn't be appeased by his own thoughts. He would have to hear what the police had to say. Closing his office door with a gentle click, he took a deep breath and stepped down the hallway towards the lounge where two policemen stood waiting for him. At least, he assumed they were police, but they wore no uniform.

"David Webb?" a full-figured man in an off-the-peg grey suit covered in crumbs (donut?) leaned his weight onto the scuffed loafer of his right foot. David had to answer quickly; the man's eyebrows threatened to weave with the shock of dark hair stretching down to meet them.

"Yes. I am he," he said in what he hoped was a humorous way.

The eyebrows relaxed a little, but only returned to a place also attended by ratty little eyes after he had completed his introduction. "Chief Inspector Lindsay, and this is Sergeant Madoc; Dyfed Powys Police."

Well I didn't think you'd be the FBI, David didn't say. "Yes? Is there news on Mari? I mean Mrs Mathias? Or is it Ms?" David's forehead creased. "I presume that's why you're here?"

"Oh yes, sir. That is why we're here." Something in the gruff manner told David it was not going to be good news. "We have been investigating all morning and are already developing a theory."

"You haven't found her, then?"

DCI Lindsay pursed his lips and glared. David wasn't sure he understood the answer. "Remind me, sir. You had your own theory, didn't you? I couldn't quite believe it when my constable told me. I thought there might be some mistake. Would you care to tell me yourself?"

Glancing at his brother, then back at the swarthy policeman, he couldn't meet his small eyes. He knew it sounded ridiculous. It had to be a nightmare, didn't it? But he had no choice but to recount his morning dog-walk with the three others in the room, which turned out to be four as when he'd finished, Sara huffed up the stairs; a barely concealed "For fuck sake, Dad," mumbled under her breath.

"A big, ape-like creature..?"

David nodded.

"You'll forgive my scepticism, sir, won't you?"

Colour drained from David's face and he stumbled forwards, supporting himself on the arm of the sofa. "It's the truth."

"Is it?" Lindsay spat. PC Madoc scribbled on a pad. "I'm not convinced. Not convinced at all."

David stood in defiance. "What do you think has happened to her?"

The stout Chief Inspector didn't flinch in David's brief display of strength. "Oh, I'm not sure you want to hear that," he sneered. "But there'll be plenty of time at the Station. Madoc?"

David's mumbled objections were lost in PC Madoc's efficient reading of his rights. "But my son. I'll have to pick him up from the bus stop."

"I'm sure there's someone else who will take care of that for you today?" Jimmy was about to object when DCI Lindsay's sniffing of the air stopped him. "Unless there's some reason *you* can't help your brother, Mr Webb? Jimmy?"

"Er, no, 'course not."

"Fine." He began marching to the front door where the silhouette of another man was clearly visible through the glass "Ah. Great timing. That's our cue to leave." He opened the door like he owned the place.

"Oh. Hello, DCI Lindsay. I didn't know you'd be here. I have a warrant."

Lindsay smiled at David. "They have a warrant," he said as he waved his colleague inside, followed by several others. "Meet my capable colleague, DI Jones." Stepping towards the door, he called out to the newly arrived Inspector. "We'll get out of your hair. Let me know when you find anything."

"How are you sure he'll find something? Shouldn't that be if?" crowed Jimmy.

Lindsay grinned. "Oh yes, sure. 'If.'"

David was pushed into the back of the awaiting car that didn't look like a police car, just a bland black Ford. The drive to Haverfordwest was twenty minutes of awkward silence. His processing went by in a blur: fingers dipped in ink and pressed firmly on a pad; cheek swabbed with a cotton pad before being shown to a typical cell.

"We'll call for you in a bit. Is there anyone you want to let know you're here? I strongly recommend you get yourself a lawyer. A good one," the custody officer chuckled. In the face of David's silence, he added. "Well, you have a think. I'll be back soon."

As the footsteps echoed down the corridor, the crushing in David's chest grew a little tighter with each step. When the metal door at the end slammed shut, he could hold it back no longer. Huge creaking sobs surged from his gaping mouth as he clawed his face with open fingers.

"Why is this happening to me?" he rasped at the room. "I only tried to do the right thing." He sobbed for himself and he sobbed for Mari. Something terrible must have happened to her for him to be in here. Had they found her? Dead? Mutilated? He shuddered. Would they ever believe his story?

As he rocked back and fore on the hard bench at the end of the room, thoughts assailed him: Mari's face covered in blood, her screams as the awful monster did what awful monsters do to their prey.

The scene he imagined horrified him but calmed him too. He would mourn Mari; he barely knew her, but she seemed nice and nobody deserved what had apparently happened to her. But he calmed, because as the prospect unfolded in his mind, it was clear: there would be clues.

Something the size of what he had seen would definitely leave proof of its presence. It was going to be a tough defence, but undeniable too.

It might take a while for an expert to declare Mari's death as an unfortunate encounter with a hitherto unknown wild animal, but it was the undeniable truth.

David fell back against the wall and waited for the investigation to plod towards its inevitable conclusion.

Chapter Eight

"**H**ow are we?" David looked around, wondering if in his despondency he'd missed someone else joining him in the small cell. "Have you thought about legal advice? You can get it free if you need, but we would like to question you."

He showed such compassion, David was immediately convinced everything was alright. "Do I need it?"

The custody officer smiled and nodded. "I'm afraid so." Drumming his thigh with his open palm, he paused after a flurry. "Well, what's it to be?"

David blinked. What should he do? He hadn't had need of a solicitor since moving here (apart from the usual conveyancing malarkey.) "I don't have a lawyer. What do you think I should do?"

The smile broadened. "Our duty solicitor will look after you, don't worry." And after further assurances from David that that was what he wanted, he disappeared with a promise David would soon be joined by his legal advisor.

"I'm afraid so," the words of the friendly policeman rang in his ears. That didn't sound like they'd found Mari alive and well, nor that they were already convinced her

demise had come at the hands, or vicious claws, of a rampant beast.

A sharp pain became the first indication of what he was doing. Removing his fingertip from his mouth, a quick glance revealed it was bleeding. "Shit!" he exclaimed.

He wedged his hands under his shaking thighs when he noticed his fingers edging back to the cave of death that containing his chattering teeth. The 'soon' alluded to for his lawyer to show up proved anything but. It must be getting dark outside, but there was no window to check his hunch.

As is usually the case with these things, it was when David had given up hope of anyone ever coming back to him that the shambling, shiny-headed presence of his duty solicitor edged through the door; not pushing it open fully in case the prisoner should make a bolt for it, and as if his tiny frame would have any chance of stopping him if he did.

"Mr Webb? Mr David Webb?" he mumbled, clutching a leather satchel type briefcase under his arm while with the other, he pushed thick frames back onto a red ridge on his nose (that looked more than deep enough to keep them in place in a gale but was somehow failing.) He stumbled over to David and presumed to sit beside him.

Plonking his case down and scrunching his nose left his hand free to be offered to his client for shaking. "Evan Jenkins," he said, remembering seconds later to add in his effort of a reassuring smile.

As he held out his small hand, almost hidden by a huge white cuff, David slowly brought his own hand to meet it. As it met the pasty palm of his legal help, the unfortunate oversized shirt made him wince. Great, he thought. I'm being represented by Harry Hill.

"What have they told you?" Evan asked his client as he bent over to retrieve papers from his case. "Do you know why you've been arrested?"

David paused before answering. Tapping his lips with an extended index finger, he considered carefully. "I know what they've said: that I'm suspected of murdering my neighbour, but I have no clue why they think that. I mean, it was me who bloody called them. Why would I do that if I'd just killed her?" he snorted his contempt.

"You'd be surprised. A pre-emptive strike is often considered the best course of defence by the guilty. And why did you say 'just killed?' We don't know she has been killed, do we? And we certainly couldn't say when. We only know when you reported it and that the police can't find her."

Evan's tone was harsher than David expected for his own advisor. "Who's side are you on?" he grimaced.

"Oh yours, of course. 'Innocent until proven guilty,' and all that. But you might as well tell me, did you do it? Have you murdered your neighbour, Mari Mathias?"

David shot his head back in astonishment. "What? No! Of course not."

Evan offered placatory palms. "Okay. I was just checking." Staring at his shoes, he gave them careful consideration before speaking again. "I probably shouldn't ask, but I feel I must. I was told you have an... unusual defence? A monster. Is that right?"

David sighed and slumped against the painted wall. "Yes," he breathed. "There was a fucking huge hairy beast hurtling towards me on the other side of the valley. *That's* why I phoned the police. I thought Mari might be in danger. I wish I bloody hadn't bothered now." Evan scribbled on his legal pad. Frowning, David carried on. "It doesn't sound like I've done any good, and I could have saved myself a whole lot of bother."

Writing what seemed like a lot more than David had said, Evan Jenkins put up his hand to prevent interruption as he mouthed the words with line thin lips. "And you're sticking with that?" he said eventually.

"I don't have a choice, do I?" David shook his head.

"Mmm-hmm," Evan added, scribbling frantically. "Tell me, is there a history of mental health problems in your family?"

David gasped.

"I'm not saying you're crazy," he crossed his eyes and stuck his tongue out from the side of his mouth. "But if you are hoping to offer an insanity plea, it will be a lot more plausible if there's a family connection."

"I don't want to pretend I'm insane! I'm innocent, and I think there's a wild creature out there. You should listen to me. People are in danger, for Christ's sake."

Evan looked offended by the blasphemy, but David was losing his patience. "Just get me out of here, will you?"

Evan smiled, what little colour remained in his face drained into his neck, the contrast of puce against white quite startling. "I'll do my best, of course." Closing his tatty briefcase, he stood abruptly and strode to the door. Turning, the courtesy of goodbye fumbled from his mouth as he disappeared from view.

"Well. That went well," David closed his eyes and banged the back of his head against the wall. "What now?"

Chapter Nine

The same smiling officer returned to escort him to *interview room one.* Leading him to a seat the other side of a wooden desk, he waited smiling at the door until they were joined by Chief Inspector Lindsay. He was accompanied by another officer; not PC Madoc, but a lady.

"We'll make introductions and get started, shall we—once your legal advisor graces us with his esteemed presence." David did his best to smile. "We already met this morning, of course," beamed Lindsay, and this is my colleague, Inspector Eleri Morgan."

They sat on the plastic chairs and arranged themselves comfortably. Lindsay loosened his tie and Eleri directed her enigmatic smile at him in what in other circumstances David might have taken as flirtation. He gulped and glanced away. When he looked back she was still smiling at him and he burned a furious red on his cheeks and neck.

"Ah here he is!" Lindsay chuckled as Evan Jenkins made his meek shambling entrance just as he had in the cell.

"Sorry. Nature called." Lindsay struggled to disguise his disgust as Mr Jenkins wiped his hands on his trousers and jerked fingers to his fly, which, in finding everything as it should be, seemed to relax him.

Stumbling chaotically to the seat next to his client, he instilled no confidence in David, but he had nothing to hide.

"You two have had a chance to talk, yes? You know why we've brought you here?"

David nodded and Evan took control adding his own mumbled "Yes, yes. We've had a little chat."

"Right, then. Let's get this started." Leaning forwards, he clicked a button on the archaic tape machine and spoke into the microphone. "Interview of David Webb on eighth of July, two-thousand seventeen. The time is..." he squinted at his wristwatch, "four forty-four." Treating the rest to an augmentation of his smile in expectation of their appreciation at the alliterative digits, he raised both palms in apology recognising perhaps now wasn't appropriate.

As his hands came to rest in front of him on the desk, DCI Lindsay's face clouded over; the 'chummy' routine abruptly over. "What happened this morning?"

David edged forward in his seat and lifted his chin so the microphone would catch every word, but before he opened his mouth to speak, Jenkins tapped his leg and whispered into his ear. "You don't have to answer that."

David glared. "I'm fine. I have nothing to hide."

Whilst DCI Lindsay now resembled a pit-bull, Eleri maintained her enigmatic gaze. Silently, she sat caressing her knee through flesh-coloured tights. David frowned unsure where to look, and the steely glare from Lindsay wasn't helping.

No-one spoke, all waiting for David. "I went for a walk with my dog. She stopped dead, growling at something. When I looked, I couldn't believe it. I thought it was an actor in a suit; you know, with all the filming that goes on around here?"

Lindsay glared and drummed his fingers in agitation. He wasn't buying any of it.

David was cross too. He was telling the truth, and if the Chief Inspector didn't like it, then he could lump it.

"Across the valley, it was; thank god! Any doubts about whether it was real disappeared as it launched itself down the hillside, trees splintering in its path."

"And then you called the police?" It was the first time he'd heard her voice as it caressed like honey in his ears. He nodded enthusiastically, but then remembered what had actually happened.

"Well. I saw Mari's car; it was parked right next to mine. But I had no phone signal, so I had to go home to call you."

"So," piped up Lindsay, "You say you saw an animal. The Pembrokeshire Panther, or The Beast of Benfro or whatever they're calling it, running towards you, and instead of calling out for your neighbour to warn her, you went home?"

David winced. It sounded bad from Lindsay's lips. "I thought calling her might bring her *into* danger."

58

"Did you? Really?" his adversary spat. Sitting back in his chair, he gestured for David to continue.

"Yes. It makes sense, doesn't it?" No-one answered. "I went straight home, phoned 999, then rushed back."

"You weren't afraid anymore?" Eleri's eyebrows twitched.

"Well, yes. But I couldn't leave Mari out there alone. Not after last time." In answer to the arched brows of his audience, David added. "I heard a panther... in the Preselis a while back. Nothing happened, but I regretted not warning some people, that's all."

"And now there's no sign of Mari Mathias," Lindsay picked up, "you are suggesting she may have fallen victim to this... beast?"

David nodded. "I know. It sounds ridiculous, right? I really hope not. She was a lovely lady; or still is," he corrected. "But if you haven't found her yet, it doesn't look very promising, does it?"

Lindsay coughed. "No, David... May I call you David?" David nodded. "It doesn't." He leaned forward in his seat again and glared into David's eyes. "What have you done with Mari Mathias?" he slammed his hand on the table. "And don't bother denying it. We've been to her house. We've read her diary."

"Her diary? What about it?"

"Getting a bit close, were you? Wouldn't she take no for an answer?"

"She flirted with me. Once. And, actually, she did take no for an answer."

"Not according to her diary she didn't."

David gasped.

"According to that she had quite a thing for you, but why am I telling you? You know all this already," Lindsay drawled. "She was getting too close and you shut her up. Didn't you? Didn't you!" He jumped from his seat and lunged across the table, saliva wetting his snarling lips.

David quivered mumbling "No, no, no."

"Interview suspended at five ten." Walking to the door, he glared back at David. "Get him out of my sight."

As the door swung back, Eleri leaned in and smiled. "He's angry because he wants the truth, that's all. You have a think about that, okay." She rose elegantly and walked through the door. The custody officer magically appeared to return him to his cell.

"What was that all about?" David turned to Evan Jenkins.

"Have a rest and we'll talk tomorrow."

"Tomorrow?" David panicked but wasn't surprised. There had been nothing in DCI Lindsay's manner to suggest anything different.

Chapter Ten

"**S**o, where is Dad?" Marcus pouted. Uncle Jimmy tried to answer with a triangle of takeaway pizza lodged in his mouth so Sara stepped in. Rolling her eyes before she had even opened her mouth her tone dripped with sarcasm.

"He's in police custody." Marcus's nose crinkled in disbelief, despite this being the fourth time he'd been told. "He might have done something exciting for a change!"

Jimmy forced a lump of cheesy bread past his epiglottis with considerable difficulty. Raising a hand to pause the conversation until he'd recovered enough to speak, with one final gulp he said, "That's not nice now, Sara. A woman is missing."

"I know! And Dad might have killed her."

Jimmy recognised her callousness for the teenage bluster it was. She could afford to be flippant because they all knew his brother wasn't capable of hurting anybody.

"What woman?" Marcus dribbled tomato sauce from the pizza base down his chin as he spoke before swallowing.

"One of your neighbours, apparently."

"And you wanna hear what Dad offered as his alibi!" Sara's eye-rolling went into overdrive and Marcus paused with another triangle between plate and mouth. "A monster did it!"

Marcus dropped the slice back on the plate for dramatic effect. "What sort of monster?"

"Oh, what do you think?"

"A panther?"

"No! This time he reckons it's a fucking bigfoot!"

"Sara! Language," Jimmy attempted to control his niece.

Marcus and Sara laughed cruelly. "We should get Mum home. Never mind a new species of Chimpanzee. A bigfoot trumps that!" Sara squealed.

David sat and stared at the wall. Things weren't getting any better and his decision to go with the duty solicitor had become one he bitterly regretted. He'd always believed if you were innocent you had nothing to fear from the Great British justice system.

But he could hardly blame them. What had seemed like a brilliant idea when he believed evidence of the creature he'd seen would be irrefutable, now showed itself to be the idiocy it had always been. What next? Suggest she may have been beamed up by little green men?

DCI Lindsay was playing a waiting game. He had been silent for at least ten minutes, occasionally prodding his chin as he leaned back casually on the horrid plastic chair.

Evan Jenkins fumbled with the buckles on his briefcase and was clearly at a loss. His advice to tell the truth, or plead insanity had been ignored by his client, and short of agreeing that a giant hairy sasquatch was a likely culprit, he had nothing else to suggest.

"I know how it looks," David broke the silence at last. "Believe me, I do. But I don't know what else I can say."

Lindsay placed his hands calmly in his lap. "Fair enough. Stick to your story. But let me tell you what I think." He leaned forward and glared at his suspect. Madoc, who had replaced the lovely Eleri in the co-pilot seat, examined his fingernails in a show of bored disinterest.

"The evidence tells a different story. Yes, there are broken trees. But there are also huge fucking diggers and forestry machines to account for them." His piggy eyes shrank to laser-points and just as intense as he focussed his venom on his suspect. "Whilst there are thousands of footprints, and lots of caterpillar track prints, there are no *big*foot prints. Surprise, surprise. So why don't you admit that you made the whole thing up? No-one will ever believe anything different."

David stared. He couldn't, but he wished he had something else to say.

"It doesn't matter," Lindsay shrugged. "I don't suppose you'll trot out that bullshit in court, and I have enough evidence anyway."

"Evidence?" David grimaced.

"Evidence?" Evan Jenkins frowned. "Why have I not been informed?"

He knew why. Lindsay was playing his cards close to his chest and he owed the lawyer no favours. Narrowing his eyes to almost invisibility to contain some of the hatred he felt for this legal advisor's willingness to hide his buffoon of a client from justice, he sighed. It was vital he had a defence. It was his right. If he was denied it, how could Lindsay put him away for a very long time; which is exactly what he expected to do?

"Allow me to enlighten you. Having established no sign of Mari Mathias, and no sign of the bogeyman, what were we left with?" No-one spoke. "Quite a lot, actually." Smiling, his eyes shone bright from their tiny holes. "We have cloth from a coat attached to Mari's car. Do you know where the cloth came from?"

David shrugged.

"Want to guess? Never mind, I'll tell you. It was from *your* coat, David. The same coat you wore when you met my officers in the wood."

"Oh yes. I remember, but I explained that! Mari had parked so close that my coat caught on her door handle. I ended up climbing through the hatchback of my car to get in!"

"Don't worry, David. There's lots more. We've had the lab reports back and they confirmed what I knew all along. That you were *inside* Mari Mathias's car."

David gasped. "I wasn't," he began to deny, but he had been, hadn't he. Not yesterday, but he had been in her car. "That was weeks ago. She gave me a lift."

"Oh, I think she gave you a lot more than that!"

David's downturned pout attempted a carefree denial, but he did care, despite having no clue what the detective was on about. The next bombshell nearly floored him.

"We found traces of semen on the passenger seat. And, yes, David. It was yours, of course."

David's mind raced. How? That was impossible. Squinting, he closed his eyes and thought back to the day of the lift. He had been pretty sozzled. Monique's involvement with Brad had just come to light and he'd had quite a few pints with whiskey chasers in The Amroth Arms. He could barely walk.

He remembered her hand caressing his thigh. The perfectly manicured nails, her voice cooing that she knew he was troubled and he didn't have to feel unappreciated. There was a twitch in his crotch at even the memory. Even now, in his fraught frame of mind, the mere memory of her turned him on. Could she have done more than stroke his leg? She must have.

"I... don't know how... I don't remember," he sighed, ashamed and afraid.

"That's a shame. Because it is a vital piece of evidence. Damning. Very damning indeed. I could show you Mari's diary. That fills in a lot of the gaps in your memory." Lindsay beamed, his widow's peak and eyebrows dancing closely on his brow.

Evan Jenkins suddenly found his voice, and despite the onslaught they had endured, decided that now was the time to assert himself. "Are you going to charge my client, or release him?"

"Thanks for bringing that up, Mr Jenkins. If you haven't already guessed, David. We are going to charge you. The CPS agrees there is plenty of evidence. Oh, and no bail will be granted, so you'll be staying with us for a while longer. Until alternative accommodation at Her Majesty's pleasure can be arranged for you at any rate."

Evan muttered his objections.

"Of course, you're welcome to appeal that decision. You know the procedure. For now, gentlemen, I bid you adieu and I'll see you in court, Mr Webb."

David couldn't breathe.

Chapter Eleven

"Won't your uncle worry if you don't go straight home?" Daryn asked, swinging a stick he'd plucked from the floor to clear the long grass like a wooden machete.

"I'll be surprised if he noticed. He's usually asleep when I get in anyway."

"Asleep?"

"Drinks himself unconscious. He's not fit to be looking after us. It's a good job we can take care of ourselves."

With a final swish of the make-shift blade, Daryn declared, "Nearly there. It's just over the crest of the hill."

The anticipation left Marcus's mouth dry. Would it be as gruesome as his friend had suggested? When he'd cornered him between lessons and told him, he had laughed it off. Now with the reality almost upon them, he was terrified.

"There!" Daryn cried as they summited the round hill at the top of H's land. "Can you see?"

Marcus squinted. He could make out the cow, but couldn't see what all the fuss was about. Laying a few yards ahead, as they rushed towards it the smell hit him before the spectacle.

"Oh my god, that stinks!"

"I know! What did I tell you?" Daryn bounded towards the carcass with gruesome glee. "I don't reckon a panther's done this."

Marcus frowned, the reason for his friend's over-excitement dawning on him for the first time. "What do you mean? You said the beast had left a body?"

"I know. But the beast is no panther."

Staring at the gory vision before him, Marcus frowned. "It looks like a panther kill to me," he objected.

Lifting the corners of his mouth in a good-natured smile, Daryn humoured his townie friend's ignorance and pointed out why he knew what he was talking about. "Look. The organs are missing, but the membrane is still intact."

Marcus stared blankly.

"*That's* exactly what a big cat would go for first! There's no way it would leave it behind."

"Maybe something startled it. You know, a farmer or something."

"No way. No-one comes up here."

"We're up here!"

"And we've never seen a living soul any time we've come, have we? Besides, it would take its best bits and hide them. That membrane would be one of the first things to go."

"So what do you think did this?" Marcus asked, already certain he knew the answer and that Daryn was trying to get in on the action of his dad's Bigfoot story. He'd sworn

68

him to secrecy, mainly because he didn't believe it himself, but Daryn had nodded as though it was a likely explanation for David's predicament.

"I don't know."

Marcus was stunned.

"But whatever it was didn't kill for food."

Marcus staggered back. "What do you mean? How are you so sure?"

Daryn shook his head. How could his friend be so unobservant? "I don't know any animal which kills for food, leaves the soft flesh but takes the lips!"

Marcus stared down at the weird lipless blood streaked face of the poor cow laying in an ungainly heap in front of him. Flies buzzed around every orifice as he peered in disbelief. "Maybe they taste really good?"

Daryn scoffed. "An animal big enough to do this to a cow and eating only the lips! Come on. That makes no sense."

Marcus pursed his mouth and nodded. "We should get a picture of this. It might help my dad."

Daryn waited for Marcus to fumble his phone from his pocket, but then suddenly he squealed. "Run. Now!"

Marcus's instincts were to object, but the terror in his friend's eyes told him not to. Bolting behind Daryn as he turned and ran, his mind contrarily remembered a story about two Ethiopians on the savannah. Upon encountering a lion, instead of running, one of the pair stops to change into his running shoes. "Don't be a fool," the first one hisses. "You'll never out run a lion."

The second man smiles. "I don't have to. I only have to out run *you*!" he says sprinting into the distance.

Marcus couldn't believe his remoteness at first, but as Daryn drew easily ahead of him, he recognised it not as callousness but as resolution to his fate.

Panting, pain in his side nearly felled him but he had to push on. His eyes squeezed out sweat dripping from his forehead as at last they reached the padlocked gate at the end of Hywel's field. Daryn vaulted it with ease, but as Marcus leapt, he fell short of the top and crashed to the ground with a thump. Scrabbling up, digging his fingernails into the rotten wood, he scrambled to the top bruising his shins as they bashed into every strut as he wriggled free.

Landing on the mud the other side, the barrier gave him the courage to glance behind him for the first time. There was nothing there, but Daryn was still sprinting fast. The stitch in his side burned as air creaked in and out of his lungs. All that time running around on *Grand Theft Auto* was no substitute for actual exercise.

Daryn finally paused as they reached the line of houses, confident they could disappear inside if whatever had chased them appeared in the distance.

"What was it?" Marcus rasped.

Daryn shrugged. "I don't know. I saw something at the treeline... I'm not sure. It was big, I think."

"You don't know! We ran for miles, and you don't know!"

"It's hardly miles. Barely a mile. And did you want to stick around and have done to you what was done to that cow?"

Marcus's fingers shot instinctively to his lips. He shook his head.

"I'm going home now. See you tomorrow," Daryn sighed, not sure what else to say.

Marcus nodded. "Seeya." Turning, he headed up the hill into 'Pen Yr Cwm' and his house, 'Valley View'. What had just happened?

As he walked, something caught his eye. A car he didn't recognise sat parked in Mari Mathias's driveway. The occupant wore sunglasses and made a poor show of disguising he was watching him.

The impulse to run to the window and demand the man come and look at the mutilated cow was strong, but he decided against it. There had been a dozen cases of dismembered cows and sheep on farms lately. One more couldn't make them believe his dad's innocence, could it?

Chapter Twelve

They were having a final bash at him before he was taken to prison, pre-court. If he cooperated, they said, maybe bail could be granted. If not, he should expect to stay on remand until his trial. He may never see the light of day again.

"But I haven't done anything."

Eleri Morgan sat opposite him now; alone. Their tactics were blatant. They'd wanted to see his reaction to a pretty woman at the first interview. Now, based on that reaction, they expected him to succumb to her girly wiles and confess. But he couldn't confess to what he hadn't done.

"Come on, David. If you tell me, I can help you. You don't want to make it worse than it is."

"How can it possibly be any worse? I'm going down for this, aren't I? A neighbour gets a crush on me. That's all you've got. And I told you the rest. What happened to innocent until proven guilty?"

"Oh, come on!" she spat. "You have motive. You had the opportunity... Your DNA is at the scene of the crime. There's literally no-one else we can say that about. And your alibi is ridiculous, I don't have to tell you that." She leaned in with a smile. "So why don't you tell me what you did with her body. You owe her that much..."

"Motive? What are you talking about? She was a neighbour, that's all."

"Was? You're certain then?"

"No!" David screamed. "No, not at all. Only from what you guys are telling me."

"So, Mari had a 'crush' on you, you say. That crush get out of hand did it? Because we know you aren't the innocent party here, don't we. Your... forensic footprint, ahem, is irrefutable. So, what happened? Threaten to tell Mrs Webb, did she?"

"No! There was nothing to tell. Nothing of any significance, anyway. I mean, I don't even remember what you're suggesting happened."

"We're not suggesting... We know."

David's shoulders hunched. "Okay. You know. But Monique wouldn't be threatened. Have you seen her? She wouldn't be threatened at all."

"Oh, yes. We've seen her. And yes, she's very beautiful. Punching above your weight there, aren't you?"

David shrugged again. His shoulders were getting quite the workout.

"I bet you worry. Her being far away, and with another man who seems, on the face of it, to be your superior in every way."

"Shut up! Fucking well shut UP!" It's what she'd wanted. He would crack if he had anything to say in this state. But

73

he was still winning because there was nothing to confess.

"And, sorry. It isn't 'Mrs Webb' at all, is it? Because she didn't even take your name, did she?"

David's head shook slowly and he whispered, "She's a well-known photographer. Her name is her brand."

Eleri grinned. "Yes of course. I wouldn't change Xerri for Webb either. Much more exotic."

"How..?"

"How do I know? Like you say. She's illustrious. It only took a quick internet search to find out more than I even wanted. It's getting so difficult for criminals to hide from the police nowadays, I almost feel sorry for you. Almost."

It must have been part of their plan. Good cop/Bad cop. It was confusing that Eleri who had played 'good cop' at their last encounter was being such a bitch to him. And now Lindsay entered the room, his current eyes juicy with hatred, any hope things were about to improve evaporated.

His first words after updating the tape-recorder of his presence, were accompanied by a violent thumping of the table in front of them. "Listen here, you little shit! I *know* you killed her, and why."

David stared back. "You can't know anything, because I *didn't* kill her!" he shrieked. "You don't even know she's dead. She might have walked to Amroth and hooked up with another drunk on the promenade… I mean apart from me." He was still shocked at yesterday's revelation.

He'd been so proud of his steadfast faithfulness in the face of severe temptation during his lowest ebb, and it turned out he hadn't resisted. He just couldn't remember, and that wasn't the same thing at all.

"Oh, she's dead, you sick bastard. And from what we found of her, you must have a hell of a temper on you!"

Blood drained from David's face and his arms fell limp at his sides. "No…"

"Didn't think we'd find her if you cut her up small enough? Well. The lab came back to us, and from bone fragments and dental records, there's no longer any doubt. You even killed her poor fucking dogs, you utter… Why? Thought them disappearing too would be a better cover story? Thought we'd think she'd gone away of her own accord? You must think we're fucking simple…" Lindsay stopped himself and pinched the bridge of his nose. Pin-prick eyes found their target as he spat, "And you, my sick fucking friend… You are going away for a very long time. The only hope you have of any type of lenience is if you confess."

Lindsay sat back, a self-satisfied smirk on his face. "Now, to be honest, at this point I don't really give a shit if I get your confession or not. I'm getting my conviction either way. I'm telling you for your own benefit; and to save the taxpayer the cost of a trial." Pushing the pad and pen towards him, he coughed. "So go on. Do yourself a favour…"

But there were no favours.

There was nothing but blackness in David's future, except for one thing...

He *knew* he was telling the truth.

Chapter Thirteen

"**L**isten carefully. Are you listening?"

The question shouldn't have needed to be asked, but Jimmy's new role as carer and guardian of who he was rapidly considering as his 'delinquent' niece and nephew distracted him from his brother's urgent plea.

"Yeah, course. Come and visit you tomorrow. Got it. Eat your bloody fish fingers, you two."

"Oh, that's what they are," Sara's sarcasm too easy to detect through the crackling prison phone line. David hoped it hid her distress at him being locked away. With a line smile and watery eye, he gulped down his fears. He had to be strong. He had to get to the truth and back to his family.

"How will I get there?"

David sighed, but then carefully forced a smile back on his face. He couldn't risk upsetting his useless little brother. He couldn't afford to give him any excuse not to come. "A bus leaves for Swansea at the end of our street. You can get on that, can't you?"

"I don't have the readies, bruv... I could use your car..?"

"Fine. Phone the insurance company. Get them to add you as a named driver. The policy is in my desk top draw, okay?"

"Yeah. Great. Thanks, man. See you tomorrow. Pick that up! I don't care if it does taste like rubber..."

He was gone. But David was sure he could rely on him to come. He had to; he had a lot more he needed to trust him with than that.

"Why are you late?" David sat across the table from his younger brother and fumed. One job, and he was late.

"That's a nice greeting!" Jimmy grinned. He had got here earlier, had trouble parking and opted for Tesco car-park—which led to temptation. After a good dose of Dutch courage (literally, as Heineken was on special offer), Jimmy felt ready for prison. He'd been here himself, of course. That's what made him feel so uncomfortable now.

"I thought it would make a nice change; visiting: seeing it from the other side, so to speak." David was being uncharacteristically unkind. The stress obviously getting to him.

Jimmy glared. "I'll go now, shall I?"

The show of strength, like any assertiveness directed at him, had David simpering and begging him to stay. "No, no. Just joking!"

"What is it you want me to do?"

David fought sarcasm threatening to spew offensively from his lips, took a deep breath and placed his hands with great care in front of him on the table. "I need to get out of here. Obviously I'm innocent, but convincing anyone else; anyone with any clout," he clarified, "that's proving impossible."

"Well, you can't be surprised. Your defence sounds like the sort of shite I'd say."

"You're right. But, in this case, it happens to be the god's honest truth."

Jimmy sat back in his chair, his fingers clasped across his stomach as he let out a whistling breath.

"What? Don't you believe me?"

Jimmy shook his head. "It hadn't occurred to me. I assumed you were pleading insanity; that the truth was too incriminating. They've been all over the house. Spent days in your office; tried to get hold of Monique—we all have. Your computer's been taken for evidence..."

"Shit!"

"Something on there?"

"Only all my work, which I hadn't finished. I won't get paid if I don't get it done soon."

"Nothing incriminating?"

David snorted. "Like what?"

"I don't know. Messages between you... pictures?"

David stood up, throwing his chair back in indignation. At an approach from the guard, he raised placatory palms and sat back down. "I'm not having an affair!" he hissed. "Not now, and not before poor Mari was killed."

"Murdered, you mean."

"No! It was that thing. That sasquatch, yeti, bloody bigfoot thing. You have to believe me. You're my only hope." In so saying, whilst looking at the dishevelled wreck sat opposite him, that hope seemed very faint indeed.

"I'll need a lawyer. A good one. Can you sort that for me?"

Jimmy nodded, but he was thinking about the beer he'd left in the car. It would be getting warm.

"But more important than that... I want you to find the creature! That beast. If you can do that, all of this," David gestured around him. "All this goes away."

"How am I gonna do that? The police have looked everywhere and found nothing."

"But they don't believe me. You can look with a better attitude. An open mind." David sat back, happy he'd at last broached what needed to be done. "Monique's still incommunicado then?"

Jimmy frowned. "I thought she was in Congo?"

David was halfway through his spluttering disbelief at his brother's ignorance when he caught the grin. "Yeah, bruv. No-one can get hold of her. When did she say she'd call again?"

David shook his head. He didn't know. His eyes clouded at the hopelessness, and at the memory of why his beloved might not be in a hurry to phone home. Her and Brad together assaulted his mind and a tear welled in the corner of his eye.

Seeing the distress, Jimmy turned up his grin, his face reddening with the effort. "Don't worry. If there's a Bigfoot in the woods, I'll find him."

"There's no *if*," David snapped.

"I'll find him then. Or her. It might be a her."

Jimmy was decidedly wobbly on the drive home. Six cans of beer didn't usually affect him. It must be the stress of the prison, he decided.

When he pulled into the driveway, the new regime of the children walking themselves from the bus stop had the pleasing extra advantage that Sara and Marcus were already inside and had begun cooking. Pleasing for all of them.

"We couldn't stand fish spears again. Spaghetti okay?"

Jimmy nodded his approval. It smelled delicious.

"How's Dad?" Marcus called out from the dining room table where he was setting the three places for dinner.

"Er, yeah. He's okay. Holding up."

"He's not still going on about a beast in the woods, is he?" Sara called over the noise of draining pasta.

"A bit," Jimmy volunteered. "I'll tell you later." By that, he meant after he'd had some food, and maybe another couple of cans, and probably a nap.

"Come on, Uncle Jimbo. You still haven't told us about Dad's chances," Marcus moaned, standing in his pyjamas ready for bed, the impulse to tell them of the cow in the field hanging on his lips.

Jimmy squinted in amazement. The bedtime routine had always been preceded by shouting and threats. Well, he couldn't complain.

"What does his lawyer think?" whined Sara. "When's he coming home?"

Jimmy relayed his afternoon conversation with their father and wished he had better vocabulary to dress it up.

"He's stuffed then. Stupid sod!" Sara slouched against the back of the sofa and folded her arms.

"You never know," Jimmy tried to smile. "Bigfoot might show his face."

"How come Dad's the only person to have ever seen him? He hardly ever goes outside. All the lumberjacks and farmers and tourists have spotted nothing, and the one time he walks Jess…"

"You're right. He seems pretty adamant though. I am going to have a look."

Marcus's legs swung back and forth in excitement. "Mum will be well jealous. Bigfoot beats Bili Ape, I reckon!" But then his foot stopped moving and his face flushed. "I'm not saying I believe him. It'd just be funny, that's all."

Sara grinned at her brother. "Mum wouldn't want to miss out on this. Imagine if it were true! Imagine if Dad hasn't simply completely cracked!"

"Yeah," Marcus's smile fell. He had to say, didn't he? He had to risk making a fool of himself. "Daryn showed me something yesterday," he blurted.

Jimmy and Sara stared at him. He was being strange. After a long pause where Marcus's face grew paler and greyer, Sara prompted him.

"You gonna tell us, or do we have to guess?"

"It was a cow."

"Oohh. Had you not seen one before?" Sara teased. "Did you miss the 'know your animals' day at school?"

Ignoring her, the memory of the stench and the weird sight, and then him and Daryn running petrified, drained the last of the colour from his face, "It was dead," he shuddered. "Its lips were gone."

The temptation to tease her brother more halted in the face of his distress. "No lips? That's weird!"

Jimmy stared. The promise he'd made to his brother to find the beast had just got real.

"You okay, Uncle Jimmy?"

"Where? Where did you see this cow with no lips, Marcus? Can you show me?"

"What, now? It'll be dark soon, and... There was something else."

Eyes staring at him, he babbled how they'd run from nothing, the sweat beading on his brow belied how scared he'd been—still was.

"Well it's obviously not nothing. There's something out there and I've told your dad I'll find it. I'll have to have a look at this cow, Marcus. Can you show me?"

Marcus nodded. He'd never seen Uncle Jimmy as anything more than the burden his parent's complained about; and a bit of a laugh sometimes. Volunteering to hunt a cow-killing neighbour-eating monster wasn't what he expected from his aberrant uncle. "In H's field."

"Where it says *'Danger, mines, keep out'*?" Sara scowled.

"Yeah," Marcus glanced at the floor then back again. "Daryn told me about the cow, so I had to go," Marcus excused, not hinting that he and Daryn went there all the time with the whim of finding secret mine shafts to underground realms.

"Where abouts?" Jimmy pressed.

"Head towards the trees. As you get to the top of the hill, the smell hits you. You can't miss it. Its organs are missing, but the membrane Daryn kept going on about was still there. He says that meant it couldn't be a panther, and whatever made the kill didn't want to eat it."

Scowling through what was making less sense by the minute, Jimmy stood to leave. "I'll go up. Take pictures. This could be just what David needs."

"But there have been loads like it already," Marcus interjected. "I don't see why this one would make a difference." It was more of an excuse as to why he'd kept it to himself, rather than a heartfelt objection

"Well, maybe I'll track it down," Jimmy grunted. "There has to be tracks. I can photograph the thing itself. You can't tell me that won't help!"

"We'll come with you," Sara's insistent voice was not to be argued with. Looking at the two males, she smiled. "Okay?"

They both nodded. Jimmy added, "But if things get dangerous, you hurry straight back, yeah? Promise?"

The pledge, broken before it was even uttered, hung in the air. They all knew this was already dangerous.

"I need to fetch something," Sara remarked. "Get your clothes on, Marky." Disappearing into the garage, she pulled a stepladder from a corner and propped it against the ceiling storage, formed crudely by boards placed over the rafters.

The space was full to bursting with boxes unopened since their move to Wales. Plans for a games room or gym looked like they'd never happen; and as for putting a car in here? No chance.

Pulling at a long leather case, when finally free from its constricting comrades, she wafted it above Jimmy's head. "Take it, it's heavy."

The shape of a gun unmistakable, so too was its feebleness as Jimmy recognised a common air rifle. The shotgun he'd hoped would appear as he unbuckled the strap failing to materialise.

"I recognise this!" Marcus cooed, walking in buttoning his jacket. "That rat we had. Remember? Dad didn't shoot it in the end, did he?"

Sara shook her head. "Never came back. Almost like it knew we planned to kill it! But we did destroy a few water melons," she chuckled, nodding to her uncle, seeing the disappointment in his eyes. "It's more powerful than it looks."

"It won't be much help against whatever's out there though," Jimmy nodded towards outside.

"I know this won't kill it, but it's got to hurt... It'll buy us escape time."

The reality kicked into Jimmy's beer-soaked brain. "I don't think you should come. I promised to look after you."

"Well, tough," Sara scorned, door already open. "We're going. You can stay here if you like."

Striding up the hill and round the little lane that snaked up to H's field, Sara watched Jess as she padded ahead, the reluctant scout. In a tight grip, she clutched the rifle to her chest and prepared for goodness knows what.

'Danger! Keep Out. Old Mine'

Sara reached the sign first. The red letters seemed unnecessary. Like overkill. The little overgrown lane didn't look inviting and Sara couldn't imagine who would be attracted to venturing over the rickety gate into the muddiness beyond. Catching sight of her brother, she shook her head. He was exactly who would breach the border onto private property, and she was sure the notice had been all the encouragement he'd needed. Old mines sounded like an invitation for adventure.

"You shouldn't come up here, you and Daryn. It's dangerous." Sara couldn't help herself.

"Well it's a good job we did. We might free Dad because of us," he said without pause, his foot poised on the first rung of the gate. Jess scrabbled under, the bottom strut squeezing the skin on the top of her head so she wore a look of surprise on her canine brow until she wriggled free.

Sara was surprised she hadn't picked up the scent of anything that worried her. She just seemed pleased to be on a walk.

"Where is this mutilated cow?" Jimmy asked, sliding in the mud at the foot of the gate and steadying himself against the green wood.

"A while yet. It's near the top of the hill."

The summit was difficult to make out in the failing light, so it was with some confusion that they suddenly reached it.

Squinting back where they'd walked, Marcus frowned. "I'm sure this is right."

But the view proved hard to match with yesterday's, the dusk giving it a different prospect. Coupled with the memory-erasing adrenaline pulsing through his veins, he wasn't entirely shocked to have made a wrong turn.

After several retracing of steps up and down the hill, Marcus was forced to acknowledge the possibility: "It's gone! It was definitely around here."

The whites of Sara's eyes were obvious even in the increasing moonlight. Marcus was sure he heard her tut-tut.

"It was definitely here! I didn't make it up. I'm not lying."

"Why would you say that? No-one suggested you were," Sara glared, her suspicion raised by her brother's prolific protestations.

Dropping to the floor, Marcus squashed his face into his cupped hands. "Fine don't believe me. I know what I saw."

"I believe you. We both do," soothed Jimmy. "The panther, or whatever, must have dragged it to its den, do you think?"

"Daryn said it couldn't be a panther. It didn't look like a panther kill."

"I said 'or whatever,'" Jimmy placated.

"What's that!" hissed Sara. Jess growled a low throaty rumble. Tail back and ears pricked, she stared at something in the woods.

A light flooded the trees, their peculiar geometric planting creating beams blinding them from its source. Feet turning one way, then another the three and Jess debated running or facing whoever it was. Surely, they must have seen them already?

A voice confirmed it, but came not from the light up ahead but from further down the hill. "What are you doing? This is private property!" The Welsh accent from the area's major landowner echoed through the night.

"Mr Jones, we're sorry, I wanted to show my uncle and my sister the cow I saw here. Did you see it?"

"There's no cow. And I told your father, before his fall from grace, that you were expressly forbidden to come onto my property."

Sara opened her mouth to defend them but H blustered on. "I shall be informing the police. I can have you arrested, you know. Now, go on. Get off my land."

"Sorry. It's my fault. I thought it might help my brother if we could get a picture of a cow clearly killed by a big animal," Jimmy deflected.

"We're all devastated by what your brother has done. Mari was such a lovely lady. We all miss her. I understand you must be shocked... your own brother... and father." H sighed. "But even the police need a warrant to intrude onto people's property, so I don't know what you think you're playing at!"

He was right. And just as he had said; the cow wasn't there, and there seemed no point hanging around trying to persuade him differently. The photo opportunity had passed.

"What are those lights, H?" Sara's voice quivered in the darkness as she pointed at the searing brightness in the trees. "What are you doing in the woods?"

H scowled. "You are on very thin ice, young lady. What I do on my own property has nothing to do with you. Now just go away, off my land, now."

"I hope you have planning permission for wherever those lights are coming from. They're very bright. You wouldn't be growing something you shouldn't, now, would you?"

What was she thinking? That he was a septuagenarian dope dealer? His scornful face told her she'd shot far from the mar and he almost looked amused. Noticing, for the first time, the shotgun resting at H's side, Sara decided against upsetting the old man further. "Okay, we'll leave. But my dad is innocent. He could never hurt a fly."

Scurrying away down the hill, they reached the gate fronting the lane and clambered over. From a distance they heard H as he yelled, "If I see any of you on my property again, I won't hesitate to call the police... It's for your own safety," he added under his breath, but Sara's keen ears still caught it; and the regret in his voice. What did he mean?

Chapter Fourteen

"Why was there even a cow in H's field?" Sara frowned before they reached the front door. "One cow. It doesn't make sense."

"Obviously it didn't live in the field on its own. The panther, or whatever," Jimmy added with a placatory glance to his nephew, "must have dragged it there."

"A cow?" Marcus shook his head. "I'm with Daryn. It can't be a panther. They're not *that* big, are they?"

"I don't know, Marcus." Picturing it, he had to concede, it seemed unlikely. A cow was a lot bigger than a gazelle.

Opening the door and flicking on the lights, he walked straight to the fridge, calling out, "Go to bed," on the way. By the time he peeled back the ring pull and sprawled on the sofa, the house had fallen peaceful and silent.

His mind whirled. Thinking about things he'd never considered creased his brow. He pressed the cold can to his head. It was too much. A week ago, he had listened to local rumours about a supposed Pembrokeshire big-cat with scepticism. Now he was seriously considering... what? The Bigfoot David says he saw? His brother was no fool. He wouldn't make it up, so why not? Shaking his head, he just couldn't believe it. Somewhere within he must do, he realised. He'd just come back from a trip to see a mutilated cow!

Maybe it was the stress, maybe it was the tiredness, or the disappointment of their failed evening venture, and most likely it was the beer, but when Jimmy tried to fall asleep to late-night documentaries on Discovery channel, he suddenly had the best idea.

"I'll call out again," the big man on the screen was saying to the night-vision camera before howling into the dark sky. "Now listen!" Seconds later, a distant call echoed back through the darkness.

It was one of the most ridiculous things Jimmy had ever seen, but his fuggy head fought through the beer and fatigue to make sense of it.

Adverts came in frequent and abundant intervals, and every time, the poorly animated face of Bigfoot roared through the screen.

Episode after episode of *Seeking Sasquatch* followed until Jimmy felt he knew the cast. Despite watching at least a half-dozen through the night, Jimmy didn't witness any compelling evidence and found his brother's testimony even more unfeasible than ever.

"If they can't find anything with all their equipment, what chance do I have?" he whistled. Unable to sleep, he crept into Marcus's room and relieved his iPad from its charging dock. He was going to do something grown-up for a change and do some research.

Hundreds of images filled the screen. Many were obvious fakes, but others were oddly convincing. We only discovered mountain gorillas a hundred years ago, and the Billi Ape his sister-in-law had gone thousands of miles in search of was only discovered as recently as 2003.

... faecal dropping three times as big as chimp dung and footprints as large as, or larger than, a gorilla's...

the wiki page pronounced. Holy crap, Jimmy scratched his chin. Monique's out looking for a bloody Bigfoot as well, just with a different name. His mind raced. How could one of those things be racing around Pembrokeshire, and how come no-one else had seen it? "That's one hell of an exotic pet," he said to the screen as the scowling face of the ape glowered out at him above the caption "lion killer."

A shudder went down his spine. Without thinking, he'd brought up the Skype page and called Monique. A rush of adrenaline rattled his heart. He needed her strength and expertise. No joy. After ringing the shrill Skype alert for a few minutes it declared no connection. Monique Xerri was off-line.

Drumming his fingers on the coffee table, he was desperate for there to be a solution. *Seeking Sasquatch* still filled the Television screen. A quick search found contact details. It couldn't hurt, could it? He felt duplicitous. Like he'd decided it was an ape hunting the Pembrokeshire hills, but he didn't know. If a creature could be discovered and photographed for the first time ten years ago, then anything was possible, wasn't it? And something weird had happened to Marcus's cow.

"You look like crap, Uncle Jimmy," Marcus observed as he poured milk on his cereal. "Didn't you sleep?"

Jimmy shook his head. "What do you know about Billi Apes?"

Marcus shrugged. "I know Mum wants to photograph them. I know they're big and scary. Why? You don't think there's Bili apes in Colby Woods?" he chuckled. The laughing stopped when he caught Jimmy's cold stare. "Oh. You do! You think a Bili ape killed that cow?"

Standing up to put his bowl in the dishwasher, he turned to his uncle. "You need to lay off the beers, Jimbo. Seriously. If Social Services knew you were looking after us pissed…"

"Watch your language!" Jimmy glared at his nephew. "I drink. I know. I have a problem. But right now, I need to help your dad. We all do. I promised." Marcus reddened. He knew he'd pushed it too far. "Anyway. You were the one convinced something bigger than a panther killed that cow."

"Yeah, but a Billi ape?"

"They call them *'Lion Killers,'*" he cut through the air with a flat hand to underline the phrase.

"But here, in Pembrokeshire."

"I'm not saying it's an indigenous fucking species!"

94

"Watch *your* language," Uncle Jimmy, Marcus grinned. They were buddies again.

"If it is one of those chimpanzees, you can forget about us finding it," Sara scoffed, tottering into the room, tying her dressing gown as she walked. "It's taken Mum years, and she's world famous at being brilliant. And you're..."

"I know: world famous for being a complete mess."

"Well, maybe not world famous," Sara grinned. "My point is, we need Mum. She has the tracking skills and the experience to not mess it up."

"I tried Skype last night, but she was offline."

"Me too," Sara admitted. "But she'll call in soon. When she does we have to persuade her home. It's the only way."

"I thought Dad said it was a bigfoot?" Marcus chimed, even saying the word seemed stupid; like it placed their experience into the realms of mythology. He understood. As preposterous as a Billi ape running around the local woods might sound, at least no-one's doubting they exist.

Jimmy drummed his fingers on the table debating telling them of his other plan. His *Seeking Sasquatch* plan. Resting his palm flat, he decided: no. They would only laugh at him, it was laughable. "We don't know what it is. That's the point."

"Yeah!" Marcus agreed, but something in the spark of his eyes said he was excited by the idea. Maybe that his dad had discovered something incredible. Jumping up, he grabbed his school bag from the hook. "Gotta go, guys. Don't wanna miss my bus!"

The front door slammed. Sara crunched on her last spoonful of cornflakes. "You need to get Dad a proper lawyer, too."

"Yeah. Of course."

"Today?"

"'Course."

Sara's chair scraped back excruciatingly. Placing her bowl on the worktop (not in the dishwasher) she strutted from the room. She was going to make a young man very happy one day, Jimmy smiled. And very scared.

"I'm going upstairs. Don't forget... Lawyer!"

Jimmy nodded, still smiling, and placed his own toast plate in the machine. Collecting his niece's bowl, tut-tutting the while. He considered his obligations. He'd phone a solicitor. Definitely. But he would need to be at his best to ensure he didn't get fobbed off with some simpleton who wouldn't understand the intricacies of this case. And having stayed up all night watching telly and Googling, he wasn't at his best now. A nap would sort him out. Just a quick snooze and he'd be right as rain.

"Jimmy! Wake up!"

Why was he woken like this so often? Scrunching his eyes open, he croaked, "What? What do you want?"

"Have you phoned the solicitor?" Sara stood over him, haughty hands on hips.

"I'll do it now," Jimmy spluttered, pushing himself up from the couch.

Sara snorted her contempt and stomped from the room. "I knew you wouldn't!" she mumbled on her way.

Leaning forward to get the phone from the table, the battery warning light was on. He debated putting it on charge and going to the kitchen to use the tethered phone. But then something drew his eye. The iPad had a message indication and the introduction made his heart race.

1 new message: Hi from Seeking Sasquatch.

Jimmy scooped up the tablet and scrolled to the emails.

'Hi, Jimmy. Thanks for reaching out to us on the team. I have to say your story sounds fascinating. Our production team thinks so too, so we'd love to come on over. It might take a couple of days to organise but we like to strike while the iron's hot –Matt'

A couple of days! What had he even said in his message? Reading back, he was surprised at his drunken eloquence. With pursed lips, he nodded to himself. "Well, that might work."

"What? Have you phoned them?"

Jimmy plastered on his best sardonic smile –it was nothing compared to Sara's own ammunition, but he used it anyway. "Just on it now, sweetie. Just doing it now."

He went through to the kitchen clutching the tablet. Local solicitor's specialising in criminal law happily took his call and he was very careful not to put them off with his brother's unusual line of defence. He could take care of that with his new celebrity buddies. "So I can tell him you'll go and see him, then? When?"

A well-spoken voice from the other end confirmed, "I or one of my team will liaise with your brother tomorrow. If there's a chance, we'll get him out," as the reassuring smarm of a Swansea firm cooed through the earpiece. Replacing the phone to its cradle, Jimmy grinned. "Good day's work. You deserve a beer!" And being in the kitchen meant there were plenty to hand.

Pausing over one of the packs he'd bought, he took only one can despite being certain he'd want more. "I can always come back. They're better cold."

Crashing heavily on the sofa, Jimmy pulled back the ring-pull on the can of lager then prodded at the remote control. The TV launched into life bringing the last watched channel, and in a bizarre turn of Déjà Vu, the same episode of *Seeking Sasquatch* was showing. Jimmy settled down to watch. Well, it was research.

By the time his nephew barged through the door with all the subtlety of a dawn raid, Jimmy jolted from sleep—again. His default response was guilt. His mind raced to find something to latch it on; which wasn't difficult—he wasn't a model guardian, or model citizen for that matter.

Another part of his brain then counter-attacked the guilt with justifications of why he was a good guy; which also wasn't difficult, because, deep down, he was. He was doing everything he could to help his brother: taking care of the kids insomuch as providing them a guardian of legal age to prevent them being put in care, at least.

He noticed every time he lost consciousness, he had the same internal struggle and sometimes the positive side needed a little lubrication, or inhalation, to gain a good enough footing to get him through the day.

Returning to the couch with two cans of lager, he grinned. He was doing the best he'd done in a while. It had started scrounging a place to stay from his golden brother, and now he was the linchpin without whom the entire Webb/Xerri family would fall apart. They *needed* him!

With his positive outlook, he debated not even opening the second can when he realised he'd already glugged down the first. But he did anyway, though as more of a celebration of his achievements than to block his negativity. And so it was no surprise when another message from the Americans appeared on the screen.

Hi, Jimmy. All sorted. We touch down in the morning and we'll arrive at yours in the afternoon; ETA 1500h.
Regards,
Dan and the team.

Wow! They didn't seem that organised when he watched them on television. *On Television*! He was going to be a TV star. He'd seen the format (oh, boy, had he!) He would be interviewed in the woods where David saw the thing. That was always the first segment of the program.

Maybe they could interview his brother too. He wrestled with his conscience for a second before deciding he would recommend that, rather than keeping the limelight for himself; it's what selfless Jimmy should do.

Knowing esteemed guests were on their way, the mess of the lounge pricked. The can in his hand hovered over the only gap on the coffee table. He should put it down and tidy up. No, he had plenty of time. It wasn't as bad as it looked. He could finish this beer and watch this episode to the end.

Chapter Fifteen

"**S**ara! Marcus! We have guests coming, help me clean this place."

Things had distracted Jimmy until he'd been forced to call upon the reluctant assistance of his young charges as soon as they had walked through the door.

"My first day back at college, and you've got me working. They're your guests!" Sara flounced around ineffectively.

"And your mess too," Marcus added.

"Yeah. Okay. I'm sorry. But these guests have come all the way from America and it's to help your dad, so buck up."

Despite the reluctance oozing from the three of them at having anything to do with housework, the house looked better to the point that when there was a knock at the door (thankfully two hours late), the American TV crew didn't turn immediately for home.

"Jimmy! Great to meet you!" beamed the now familiar face of Dan Castle.

Jimmy stared, awestruck before eventually offering a limp hand to shake. "Sorry about the state of the place.

Being a guardian is new to me and I'm still finding my feet."

Sara rolled her eyes.

"Looks great," reassured Dan. "Let's get out to these woods then, shall we?"

Jimmy couldn't hide his shock. "Don't you want to rest? Have a sit down after travelling for so long?"

"You can sleep when you're dead, Jimmy. We need to get moving. You want to help your brother, don't you?"

Their energy was unbelievable and contagious. Just what Jimmy needed in his life. And when he stepped outside, it was like stepping into Hollywood; cameras pointing at him as he shook hands with the rest of the team. He felt most star struck when the mighty hand of Cliff 'Big Man' Miller gripped his own. A smile from 'team sceptic,' Beth, melted him into a simpering mess.

As he was shown into the back of one of three large and impressive four-wheel-drives, he thought whoever had hired these might have overdone it. Sara and Marcus hovered until they were included in the trip, despite Jimmy's hesitancy.

"It's their dad who's in trouble over this, Jimmy. It'll make great TV! Bring the dog, too," Big Man boomed.

Jimmy rolled his eyes. He could see it now. His face on the cutting room floor. How could he compete with Sara, busy blossoming into an even more beautiful version of her mother? Even Jess would get more airtime than him.

After the two minute journey, they turned onto the narrow lane that led through Colby Woods. Wincing at every turn, it was obvious the Americans weren't used to such narrow roads back home. When they pulled into the manicured car-park a minute later, they guffawed.

"You sure your brother saw a 'squatch here? It's a helluva lot closer to civilisation than your self-respecting bigfoot normally likes."

Jimmy smiled. "I don't know if I believe it. But my brother, David, is sooo sensible. I'm the flaky one. He's an accountant for god-sake."

"You said your sister-in-law is that famous photographer, Monique something..?" Dan asked.

"Xerri. That's right."

"Why doesn't she help you? Why call us?"

"She's way down deep in the middle of the Congo,"

The Americans frowned and Jimmy reddened at his rendition of the 'Um Bongo' advert from the eighties.

"It seems stupid," piped up Sara, "but if anyone can help my dad, it's you guys." Her smile was irresistible, but the team seemed unmoved.

"Well, we're here now, so of course we're going to investigate," Dan assured.

"Definitely," Big Man's voice echoed through the woodland. "Look at that dog!"

All eyes turned to the back seat where poor Jess sat trembling in a puddle of pee.

"Eww, gross!" Sara pouted.

"That's good enough for me. Our four-legged friends don't lie."

Milling about while the first shots were set up, Jimmy was surprised how organised these fly-on-the-wall documentaries were. It took a lot of planning to be spontaneous, so it seemed.

"Right! We're ready to interview you, Jimmy!" Dan hollered through the throng of cameramen and directors. "And you two, and the dog."

Jess cringed round Sara's legs and whined. Patting her soft head, she cooed, "I didn't believe it, but she sure is spooked."

The springer spaniel trembled in eerie stillness as everyone stared. "Okay," Big Man's voice broke the silence. "Let's carry on."

Jimmy couldn't show them where David had seen the 'Bigfoot,' none of them could. Because they hadn't really been listening. Faces reddened as their disloyalty to their father and brother's predicament was all too evident.

Frowns grew on the visitors' faces. The Webb family's fifteen minutes of fame stood on shaky ground. They set up the usual format: Big Man trekking into the distance to give a sense of scale. It was pointless as none of them could say, "Oh, yes. The creature stood taller than Cliff."

"You can visit my brother on remand. He'll tell you what he saw."

"Yes. That sounds great," declared Dan with a clap of his hands. "You guys can get off home. We'll stay out here and do our investigations."

"Did you tell them about the cow?" Marcus panicked.

Grateful for the shoehorn back onto the programme, Jimmy jogged backwards to maintain eye-contact. "Yeah. There's been lots of mutilated cows and sheep for weeks, and Marcus saw one yesterday."

"Its lips were removed. My friend said he knew it wasn't a panther because of it."

"Panther? You don't get panthers here, do you?" Beth asked crinkling her nose.

"Some people think there's one prowling around; escaped from a zoo, or an exotic pet," Jimmy explained.

"Right. Thanks. But eating a cow's lips doesn't sound like our type of situation. Interesting. Very weird." The words didn't match the face. "We'll have to get back to you on that one." Turning away, a crew member guide them back to the car, and the stars of the show faded from view.

Jumbling into the car, they sat in silence awaiting their driver to walk round.

"Well, that was a waste of time," pouted Marcus, arms folded in the back of the car. "They're not going to find anything, are they?"

Jimmy's lips pursed at Sara's enthusiastic response. Ruffling Jess's ears, she cooed, "You saw the sasquatch, didn't you Jessie wessie woo? You saw the nasty beastly

Bigfoot." Jess licked her face, loving the attention. "And you did a little whoopsie in the nice car, didn't you."

The American driver hauled his bulk into the car and caught her eye in the rear-view mirror and grinned at her. "Don't worry about that. It's just a hire car, darlin'."

Jimmy wasn't sure that was appropriate to say to his sixteen-year-old niece, but she seemed to like it.

Pulling into David and Monique's drive after the short drive his low rumbling voice said, "We'll be back tomorrow to show you if there's any footage, okay?" he said as they stepped out of the car. Hustling into the house, Jimmy was grateful when Sara suggested frozen pizza for dinner, and even offered to cook it.

The bright red green and yellow of the bubbling pizza sat in contrast to their quiet thoughtfulness as they ate what had become a sombre meal. Hopes pinned to something as ridiculous as trying to prove Bigfoot not only was real, but was living in Pembrokeshire, left little to say. When more than half the pizza was put in the fridge, they spent the evening unusually together in the lounge.

The film they chose drifted over them, not one of them taking it in, and when the closing credits scrolled down the screen, it was as good a signal as any to go to bed.

"Night…" Sara got up first to leave, then Marcus, leaving the 'grown-up' to lock up.

"Go and do wee-wees, Jess," he prompted her from her slumber in her bed. She wagged her tail and stretched. Ambling to the door, she stopped dead. Hackles up, she growled a low growl and backed into the kitchen. "Go on, Jess. You need to go out for a wee." But he wasn't about to go out himself and call her outside.

Heart thumping, images flooded his mind of limbs ripping from bodies as ferocious claws and teeth did their worst. "Well, you better not mess in the house." Wagging a finger at the old dog, in response, she twitched her tale in steady gratitude.

Jimmy locked and bolted the door and climbed the stairs to bed. He already knew sleep was going to be impossible, but he would try. And he'd pray that in the morning, the *Seeking Sasquatch* team would report this nightmare to be all over.

Chapter Sixteen

"I can't sleep." Marcus creaked open the door and slunk into his sister's bedroom. His heart raced at realising she wasn't there. "Sara!" he hissed before, with a shudder, he bolted from the room.

"Uncle Jimmy! Sara's gone!"

Jimmy wasn't asleep, but he was still groggy; an almost permanent state of his being. Rubbing his eyes and propping himself on bent elbows, he scowled at his nephew. "What do you mean, gone?"

Gasping, he spluttered, "She's not in her room. I don't know where she is."

"She's probably in the bathroom or getting a drink."

Marcus looked sideways as his foolishness in not contemplating the obvious caught up with him. "I couldn't sleep. Can you check with me?"

With an annoyed sigh, Jimmy threw back the covers and stomped over to the door. "Okay. But if she is just in the bathroom…" He didn't finish the thought. What did he mean? If she wasn't being mauled by an eight foot hairy beast, he'd be cross?

Gently rapping the door, there was no response. "Sara? Are you in there?" Shrugging, he turned to Marcus. "You check downstairs, I'll go up to the attic floor and see if she's up there."

Marcus pivvered from one foot to the other.

"Okay. We'll both check together."

Before they'd taken a step down stairs, Sara's quivering voice beckoned them from above. "Up here!" she hissed. "You gotta see this."

Hauling themselves up the steep staircase using the handrails, they joined Sara at the top. The boarded attic was complete for plans to be an observatory (to take advantage of Pembrokeshire's dark skies), all it needed was a telescope.

"What is it, Sara?" Jimmy asked, trying to add an air of authority.

"Shhhhh!" Sara spat, turning sharply. "Look."

Craning around the Dorma window, the two followed Sara's gaze. What would they see? A sasquatch, large as life and ready to rip them limb from limb? The Pembrokeshire panther, prowling in the moonlight?

It was neither, but what met their gaze made them gasp. Standing in the middle of the road, huddled over his cane and staring an unblinking stare right back at them, was 'H.'

"What's he doing?" Jimmy demanded.

Sara shrugged. "He's been out there for ages. Just glaring at me." Tearing herself away from the window, she sat cross-legged on the floorboards. "I couldn't sleep so I came up here wondering if I might see something. I know, I know…" she shook her head without completing *what* she knew… that she was foolish? Because after Jess's reaction in the woods, no-one could argue that.

"Mr Jones was already in the road. He noticed me and hasn't stopped staring up here since. What are you doing?" Sara panicked as Jimmy slid open the window.

"I'm going to tell him to piss off," Jimmy snorted. But in reality he was far more respectful. "Everything okay, Mr Jones?"

'H' just glared with a silent intensity.

The three of them jerked their heads as, in the distance, a blood-curdling shriek echoed through the night.

"What was that?" Marcus cried, clinging onto Sara's arm.

Jimmy smirked, proud to be the brave one. "Big Man. He does that to call out to 'Squatches." His smirk dropped as another screech resonated through the valley; much, much closer.

With eyes wide, Jimmy forced a reassuring smile to his lips. "Peacocks, isn't it?" but the look they shared showed none of them thought it was for even a second.

Marcus still looked out of the window and Sara and Jimmy squeezed in beside him. Still gawping up at them, a scowl of disgust creasing his brow, 'H' slowly shook his head. Turning away at last, he ambled along the road, head still shaking as he went.

"Weird," Jimmy was the first to speak. The siblings nodded but no-one wanted to leave the attic to return to bed. The increased height gave a feeling of safety; some extra time to contemplate their fate should the monster of David's encounter find its way into the house.

Exhaustion claimed their consciousness sometime before dawn, and when Sara bolted awake after ten, she was cold and her neck was stiff. Holding her breath, she strained to listen before daring to move. Nothing. Silence.

With a sigh, she pried herself from her brother's embrace. Laying him gently on the beanbag they'd rested on together, she smiled as she glimpsed Jimmy. Her uncle's ability to sleep was legendary, but his face pressed against the window still made her chuckle. He seemed to have adhered his cheek to the glass with a stream of saliva.

Easing herself down the steep staircase onto the landing, Sara went into the bathroom and showered before venturing downstairs to cook breakfast. As she had suspected, the smell of bacon wafting through the house was sufficient to bring the others to life once more.

They munched heartily, joking about their impromptu attic pyjama party, hesitant to mention the reason they'd been up there in the first place. Jimmy was first to approach the topic. "Mr Jones was acting weird, wasn't he?" he said with a pseudo-carefree smirk.

Sara and Marcus nodded. With lips pressed together, Marcus squinted, reluctant to go on. "Do you think it could have been peacocks we heard last night? It was really close."

"Well old 'H' wasn't bothered, was he?" chimed Sara. "He's not stupid. Would he stick around if there was some sort of monster in the woods? I don't think so." She bit down hard on some crispy bacon to punctuate her judgement.

"I think we must have been a bit on edge... maybe didn't make the best judgement. But, don't forget: we *want* there to be a bigfoot out there, don't we? For your dad's sake."

Marcus nodded. "Yeah, I know. But it is pretty scary."

It was. If they allowed themselves to admit it, it was terrifying, but it still had the distant 'happening to someone else' feel to it. It was an uncomfortable thought that that distance might be considerably shortened in their search for the truth.

"When are the Americans due to report back?" asked Sara

"I don't know." Tomato ketchup dribbled down Jimmy's chin. He cuffed it with his shirt. "I suppose I would have expected them by now. They've probably got to review their footage and stuff, I guess."

"Do you think they found anything?" Colour drained from Marcus and he flinched, anticipating the reply.

Jimmy shrugged. He'd never been so ambivalent in his life; and it was a life full of uncertainty. "I hope so, I guess."

Sara glared as she stood up to clear her plate. "Of course we hope so. I didn't believe Dad at first, I'll admit it. But we know what we heard, and so did Jess."

"How is Jess? She didn't want to go out to the toilet last night."

With a thud of her heart, Sara realised she hadn't seen her since last night. "Jess! Jess!" Running to the back door, she threw it open and yelled her name over and over.

"Sorry, Sara. I just assumed she'd gone up to your room…"

Sara stared at Jimmy and darted from the room. Leaping two steps at a time she flung open her bedroom door. She wasn't on the bed. "Shit!" Gasping for breath it took a while to detect the whimper. Bending down, she peeped under the bed. Weeping with relief, two amber eyes looked out at her from the darkness. "Oh, Jess. Thank god, you're okay. Jess?"

She'd never seen her like this. "Oh, my goodness. You're shaking." Hauling her out by her collar, the stinging odour of urine hit her. "Oh, Jess!" The poor spaniel quivered in her guilt. "It's okay, sweetie. It's okay."

Jess's ears slowly returned to the top of her head and she dared a solitary wag of her tail. Jimmy had said she wouldn't go outside, and who could blame her. Sara stroked her head, leaned in and kissed her muzzle. "I believe you, Jess. If you think there's something out there to be afraid of, then there must be."

113

"You found her! Thanks for telling us. You're not the only one who was worried," Marcus sneered.

"Sorry. But look at her, Marky. She's absolutely pissing herself... literally."

"I can smell it! What's wrong with her?"

Sara scowled. "What do you think? She's frightened, isn't she!"

Jess followed them downstairs. With company, she shuffled into the garden and squatted. It was probably more for show, her bladder had been emptied sufficiently upstairs.

"Sara, Marcus!" The call came from the front room where Jimmy was peering through the blinds. "They're here."

Chapter Seventeen

"**S**o, you definitely think there's something out there, then?"

"Oh, yes. I can hardly believe it, in such a small woodland. We said, didn't we," Dan nodded to Big Man, Cliff, and Beth, "when we looked at the map that there was *no way* there'd be anything of any size living here, but there's a 'squatch' out there for sure. It answered Big Man's calling and everything!" he enthused.

The grin on Jimmy's face threatened to cut his face in half. The delinquent little brother had saved the day. And quickly, too! David would be so relieved. They could go and tell him. It would be great for him to get some of the limelight from Monique for a change. The boring stay-at-home accountant vs. world renowned photographer and primatologist Monique Xerri! Jimmy chuckled to himself. She'll be so jealous. While she's getting pictures of a new strain of Chimpanzee, her husband and her brother-in-law have confirmed the existence of bloody Bigfoot right by their house.

"Can we go and visit David? He's going to be stoked," Jimmy grinned at the crew.

A look passed between the Americans. Dan grinned. "Already been. We got the footage we needed this morning."

"Oh," Jimmy sighed, raking sweaty fingers through his greasy hair, lop-sided smile lighting his clammy pallor. "I thought you'd want me there. I was the one who contacted you."

"Oh, sorry Jimmy. We're on a tight schedule, you know?"

"Yeah," Big Man's voice boomed. "Thanks, Jimmy. It's been great. I'm really glad we came. *Totally* worth it."

"You're going?" Jimmy's hands went from cupping his skull to a protective position in his lap. It wasn't meant to be like this. It all seemed so rushed.

"'Fraid so. But, here. Let's show you what we got."

Jimmy, Sara and Marcus huddled around Matt's laptop and watched a grainy version of the usual *Seeking Sasquatch* format. Without ad-breaks, the footage seemed even shorter.

"That's just you rushing through trees in the dark," Sara's caustic voice filled the silence when the video finished.

"We heard your 'squatch. We went after it."

"And it answered my howling. You heard it, right?" They nodded.

"Did you… Did you get any pictures?"

Dan wasn't happy with the lack of gratitude he was feeling. "You don't just get pictures of Bigfoot. You know that! Everybody knows that."

"But you said you're going. My sister-in-law; Monique Xerri?" It wasn't clear if her infamy was familiar to them. Their blank faces suggested not. "She's spending literally months in The Congo to shoot photos of an animal we already *know* exists..."

"Oh, we know Bigfoot's real," boomed Big Man. "Seen him with my own eyes plenty of times."

"Well, wouldn't it be incredible to photograph him? I thought that was the whole point of your program?" Marcus turned away with a shake of his head.

"Yeah, it would be," Dan nodded. "Of course."

"Well, *this* could be your best chance. Like you said, the woods here are much smaller than what you're used to. I'm sure you could track him down with your skills. Wow, this could be amazing, couldn't it? Don't go yet," eyebrows arched, Jimmy tried to hold Matt's gaze.

"Sorry fella," Dan insisted. "We got budgets and schedules. We came pretty close last night, but I don't think more time is gonna get us anywhere."

"Of course it will." Jimmy leaned forward and perched on the edge of the sofa. "Nothing great is ever achieved easily. You have to give it time."

Dan sighed. "Don't forget, Jimbo, no-one else, apart from your brother, has ever reported a single sighting. Our Bigfoot must have somewhere to hide, and he'll be on to us now. They're plenty smart, 'Squatches. He won't come out again 'til we're long gone. Trust me."

They had no choice. Was the brief footage of the apparent answering of Big Man's calls enough evidence to get David out of prison? Jimmy didn't think so. "But what about my brother? We need more than that for people to believe his story."

"People'll believe what they wanna believe, son. Can't change that. *We* know the truth," Big Man drawled.

Jimmy rolled his eyes. He avoided catching Sara's expression for fear of exploding with the slightest encouragement. "But we *need* them to believe. My brother is relying on us. Come on, don't let us down."

"That's it. I'm outa here! Telling us how to do our goddam job." Cliff Miller slammed a huge hand on the coffee table, threw his chair back and stormed from the room, the front door slamming in his wake.

"You've upset him. You didn't oughta have done that," Dan also stood to leave. "We never promised to get you evidence. I'll write a statement, I'm sure Big Man will, too, if I calm him down. Do you think that will help?"

Jimmy wiped a tear from his eye. What had he expected? He'd seen the show enough times. This was how every one of them ended; with nothing but misplaced enthusiasm. "Okay, thanks. It might."

The drive to Swansea was taken in silence. Sara gazed from one window, and Marcus the other. Jimmy gripped the wheel carefully obeying the speed limit. For some reason, he hadn't quite got around to changing the insurance policy for the VW, so *technically* he was driving illegally. Of course, he was perfectly prepared to pretend he was David; he knew all the relevant information to be convincing if they got stopped.

Arriving at the Tesco car park, grateful they hadn't attracted unwanted attention, the three approached the prison and went to the usual desk for visitors.

When they arrived, they were shocked to learn he wasn't alone. "There's already somebody with him," the uniformed lady looked up from her screen to greet them. "But you can wait. I don't suppose they'll be long."

Jimmy frowned as he turned to face his niece and nephew. Shrugging, they took their seats as directed.

"Who else would visit Dad," Marcus said with a tilt of his head.

The answer came quickly when a large man in a sharp suit and sunglasses exited just before they got the nod from the desk that they were free to go in.

"It must be your dad's new lawyer," Jimmy grinned. "Hey, wait up!" he called after the stranger.

The big man paused. "Yes. Can I help you?" It wasn't the Swansea accent he'd expected. The large man spoke with Big Man's American bass.

"You were visiting David Webb?"

"Sure. Who wants to know?"

119

"I'm Jimmy… James Webb; David's brother. Are you his new lawyer?"

The man chuckled. "No. But you could say I gave your brother some much-needed legal advice."

"What do you mean?"

The big man squared up to Jimmy and glared at him. Removing his sunglasses seamlessly. "You better hope you don't get to find out." Replacing his Ray Bans, he plastered an all-American, perfect teeth smile onto his tanned face. "Now. You have a nice day." Patting Jimmy's arm demonstrated his superior strength perfectly. Sauntering from the prison doors he disappeared without looking back.

"Was it?"

Jimmy's mouth creased at Sara's question.

"Was it Dad's lawyer?"

Jimmy shook his head. "No. I don't know who he was. He was American, and he wasn't friendly. I assume he's here with Dan and Big Man and the team. He said he'd given David some 'legal advice' and then threatened me."

"Threatened? How? What did he say?" Sara scowled in the direction the man had been.

"It was more *how* he said it, really."

"It'll be a non-disclosure agreement, I should think. Although there wasn't really much for him not to disclose," Marcus nodded sensibly.

"That makes no sense. We were the ones who called them," Sara objected.

"Well, technically, *I* called them," Jimmy grinned. "But I take your point. *We* didn't have to sign anything. Why would your dad?"

"But it was Dad who actually saw it," Marcus's voice got higher in his angst.

"Yeah, I suppose. Why don't we go and ask him?"

Standing to go into the visiting room, Marcus frowned. "I've seen him before, I think. When I ran from H's field after seeing the cow with, Daryn. He was parked in poor Mari's driveway. I'm sure it was him."

Without pausing, Sara answered, "Must be a researcher or something. It makes sense, doesn't it?"

They all shrugged. Nothing made sense.

Chapter Eighteen

"**M**y god, bro. You look terrible!" David's wan smile peeped out from greasy fronds of hair. His eyes were red and puffy. "You bin crying?"

The smile broadened and the effort was obvious. "No. I'm fine. It's the lack of fresh air, that's all."

"They have to let you see the sky. They never kept me locked up. You wanna say something. You want me to say something?"

Sara stepped in knowing this would get them nowhere. Uncle Jimmy could be slow sometimes. Leaning over the table, she hugged her father.

"Oi! Stop that. No touching!" A prison officer glared from across the room. Sara gave a final squeeze before letting go and mouthing 'sorry.'

"Who was the man? He said he wasn't your new lawyer."

David's pupils contracted and his cheeks reddened. "Man? What man?"

"He left just before we came in."

"Yeah. He threatened me; kind of. Said he'd given you 'much needed legal advice.' And said I better hope I never found out what."

David frowned, tapping his index finger on his lips. "Just before you came, you say?"

"We thought he was from the *Seeking Sasquatch* team. You know, getting you to sign a non-disclosure agreement, or something?" Marcus volunteered to fill the uncomfortable pause.

David grinned. "I was just kidding. Yes. That's who it was. A non-disclosure agreement. You got it bang on."

Marcus frowned. Why was Dad acting so weird? He nodded and smiled. It must be hard in here.

"Aren't you going to ask what they found, Dad?" It was Sara's turn to scowl.

Jimmy launched in without invitation, but after describing Jess's distress and Big Man's calling, he was left floundering. It had all come to nothing.

"Maybe it wasn't a Bigfoot. It does seem a bit far-fetched, doesn't it?"

The gasp from the other three attracted irritated glances from around the room.

"What do you mean? You were so certain. You told me your defence rested on me proving it."

David leaned forward, a cloud hung over him as he stared at his brother. "But no-one's ever going to fucking believe it are they? People like these clowns from across the pond have been trying for years. How are *you* gonna get enough evidence to persuade a jury?" he glared at the three of them across the table. "Eh? Tell me!"

"Mum!" Sara and Marcus cried in unison. "She could track it down and get the photos. People would believe her. She's got bags of credibility."

"No!" David hissed. "Leave your mother out of this." He took a long deep breath. "I must have been mistaken. There can't be a bigfoot in Pembrokeshire. It's far too small. I obviously imagined it."

They sat in silence for an excruciating minute as they all tried to fathom what was happening.

"So what about your neighbour? What happened to her? You're not saying you did kill her, are you?" Jimmy's mouth stayed open when his lips stopped moving.

"No, of course I'm bloody not!"

"Well what, Dad? What are you saying?" Sara's voice cracked as Marcus stared at the floor.

"Oh, I don't know what I'm saying. It's all too much. It's too much."

David's open hands flew to his face and he rocked in his seat.

"Oh my god, Dad. You're not fine, are you!" Sara stroked his arm. Marcus's moist eyes strained to stay on the distraught figure of his distressed father as he rued all the times he's talked back and rolled his eyes.

"Don't worry, Dad. We'll get you out."

Colour drained from David's face and as his clammy fingers clutched theirs. "Leave your mother be. Promise me?" Coal eyes implored them and they nodded their agreement.

"Okay. If you say so."

"I do. I really do."

Waving as they walked from the room, the pale image of David's face etched in all their minds.

"Why doesn't he want your mum to know, do you think?" Jimmy shook his confused head.

"He's embarrassed. She's out gaining fame and fortune and he's in this mess," Marcus spoke with surprising clarity. "If the Americans had found something, things would be differed. I suppose he figures if they can't, what chance do we stand?"

"Yeah, but Mum. She'd be thorough. If she even thought there was an undiscovered species on our doorstep, she wouldn't waste her time on bloody Bili Apes," Sara fumed.

"But we can't tell her," Jimmy shrugged.

"Yeah, right," Sara scoffed.

"But your dad..."

"Like Marcus says, he's embarrassed. But did it strike you he was thinking clearly?" Jimmy shook his head. "Well then. Mum's our best hope, and the sooner we can get her home, the better."

Sara pressed send on her phone for the countless time since they'd returned from Swansea Prison a week ago.

"Mum. Come home. Dad needs you…" She'd gone into great detail in her first message, and now she was executing 'virtual nagging.' Actual nagging was a technique that had worked well for her in the past: she'd gone skiing with the school, had the latest iPhone and generally did whatever she wanted.

But she knew from the little icon on her screen that the messages were not even being seen. How could she achieve her aim this time when it was so much more important? "You're going to have to find her, Jimmy."

Jimmy choked on the can in his hand. "Don't be silly. How can I do that?"

"I'm not being silly," Sara glared. "I can't exactly go, can I? And neither can Marcus, obviously. You know how schools are, nowadays. If I miss more than a day, the truant officer will visit and we'll all be in trouble. And I'm sure you don't want to send a defenceless sixteen-year-old girl into the ravages of the jungle, do you?" She fluttered her long lashes and smiled. "No. You'll have to go and find Mum."

Jimmy's pale complexion turned almost blue as his brain tried to fire up its well-used excuses engine. But he had nothing in reserve. If someone couldn't get the evidence that there might, just, conceivably, be a wild animal capable of killing someone living in the local forest, then his brother's fate would already be sealed.

"I've only ever been to Ibiza. That's not going to be much preparation for Congo, is it? I don't even know if my passport's up to date."

Sara pouted her pretty lips. "When were you last out there, in Ibiza? It was only a few months ago, wasn't it?"

Jimmy had to concede, and when they rummaged through the scruffy little bag he took from sofa to sofa, his dog-eared passport was in its usual pocket. There were another five years until it needed renewing.

"That's settled, then," Sara kept up the pressure. "When will you go?"

Jimmy gulped. "We should give your mum more time to answer. She'll be somewhere with signal soon."

"No, Uncle Jimmy. You saw how Dad was. If his trial starts without Mum's help, he has no defence. He'll go down for this and he hasn't done anything."

"How will we pay for a ticket? Where would I stay? And how on earth could I find Monique in the jungle?"

Sara grinned. These were objections she could cope with. She'd long-since stored her dad's card details to pay for online shopping. The rest would just take a little research.

Chapter Nineteen

"What do you mean, he won't see us?" Sara demanded of the prison guard. It had taken weeks to get the immunisations from the doctors and most of that time to arrange a travel plan.

Monique had details of her contacts and special permissions to enter the Bili forest; somewhere the British Foreign Office "Advises against *all* travel."

Uncle Jimmy had been understandably wary. But whilst Sara was fond of her uncle, she considered if the dangers were okay for her mum, then he should consider it an honour. Visiting her dad today was supposed to be the final push.

"If David can't even be bothered to see us, why should I bother to venture thousands of miles to war-torn Africa?"

Sara sighed. "Are you sure he won't see us? You've been really clear who we are?"

The guard's sympathy was waning as he struggle not to gaze at the ceiling and sigh. "Yes. Completely clear," he breathed. "You're welcome to try another day. Perhaps you should call first? Save yourself a wasted journey." To underline the end of their conversation, the guard hopped from his chair and disappeared from view. Sara imagined him hiding in a store cupboard until he was certain they had left.

"Come on. There's no point wasting more time."

"Really?" Jimmy was stunned. "You're just giving up?"

"We're not giving up. We're getting on. He's obviously in a bad way, and who can blame him? That's why we have to make sure we give him the best chance."

As they walked, Jimmy's mouth turned down.

"What? Are you having second thoughts?"

Jimmy laughed a nervous laugh. "No. I'm not having *second* thoughts. I'm having third, fourth, and fifth thoughts!"

Sara leaned in and hugged him. "It's a cool thing you're doing."

Jimmy felt the warmth of her approval emanate from his heart. The wave of pride just reached his lips where it faded like a ripple on a pond reaching the shore.

"… What else are you going to do? Sit on your arse drinking cans and smoking weed? If a *girl* can do it, then big, strong Uncle Jimmy can do it… can't he?"

Jimmy stopped in his stride. Her words hit home. What else was he going to do? His life was a waste of time. If he could help his brother, he'd be helping his niece and nephew and sister-in-law too. Not to mention his doting parents. If he could help David and he didn't take the chance, they'd never forgive him.

She was a master, wasn't she? From a well-timed hug and follow-up acid words, Sara had done a number on him. But far from reeling on the ropes, he felt excited!

He could save the day. He could be everyone's hero. Finally his life had a purpose.

"Help me pack a bag, Sara. I'm going to Congo!"

Chapter Twenty

As his daughter had alluded, David was *'in a bad way.'* Since the Americans had visited, he'd been a shadow of his former self. And as his former self existed in the shadow of his infamously talented wife, he was in a very dark place indeed.

He'd experienced hope briefly when they barrelled in, but they soon made it clear that, while they believed him, that's as far as it went, or was ever likely to go. And their belief was not about to convince anybody that mattered of his innocence.

So when the other man came, David was already primed to give up all hope; he supposed they planned it that way.

"You've another visitor," the guard had told him. It would be his family this time, he was sure. But it hadn't been. He had assumed, at first sight, and further when he heard the distinctive southern American accent, that the man was with the *Seeking Sasquatch* team. For a moment he'd even allowed promise to prick the back of his eyes.

And in a way he was; with them, that is.

"So, why don't you tell *me* what you saw?"

David frowned. "I don't know who you are."

"Nathan Dale. I told you." The big man shrugged, his tailored suit accommodating the move like a second skin.

"But who is Nathan Dale?"

He sighed and flashed white teeth across the table. "I have to be honest, I was hoping not to say, but I haven't really come with a cover story so I'm gonna level with you." Elbows bent, palms flat on the table, Nathan leaned in, and in a hushed tone said, "I'm with the FBI."

David snorted and blew a laughing raspberry through pursed lips. He stopped when the humour wasn't reciprocated. "You're serious. Why?"

Still leaning in, Nathan lowered his voice. "You ever watch that show?"

"*Seeking Sasquatch*?"

Nathan nodded. "Yeah. You ever wonder why they don't find one?"

David looked away before taking Nathan's gaze again. "I suppose I thought because there's no such thing. Until a few weeks ago anyway."

"And now?"

"I don't know," David shrugged. "They talked a good show. I did wonder, if they were so sure there was a Sasquatch in Pembrokeshire, why they wouldn't want to stay and get some footage. Proof."

"Exactly. Why don't they?" Nathan sat back and folded his arms and grinned.

David waited a minute until it was clear no further information would be forth-coming without further prompting. "Well, why don't they then?"

"Ha. I thought you got it then, my friend. Allow me to explain."

No-one's stopping you, David thought.

"I don't let them."

David gasped.

"Well, not *me* exactly. My organisation doesn't let them, but it's me who follows them around."

"Why?"

"Why ja think?"

"Oh!" David nodded along, it slowly seeping in. "You know they're real, and you're covering it up."

Nathan clapped his huge hands together. "Now I'm not going to confirm or deny that, but let's just say we have an understanding." His smile was intense. Pupils turning to pin-pricks, he snarled, "We *do* have an understanding, don't we, David?"

Colour drained from David's face and he nodded in rapid jerks.

"Just so I'm crystal clear. I will not allow evidence of any sasquatch, yeti, bigfoot, or whatever to surface."

"Why," David quivered.

"Do you think I can tell you that? I just told you I can't allow it, and you think I'm going to fucking tell you. Man!" He snorted through his nose forcing tantric air into his lungs as he opened and closed his fist a few times.

"As you seem particularly slow on the uptake; Jeez, they told me you were smart—some big-shot accountant; I'll spell it out. Say what you want about what happened in the woods. Say whatever it is you think happened to your neighbour. But I warn you: if you're too convincing and people start to believe you, I will shut you down. You understand?" Nathan's deep voice now resembled more of a growl. "So, if you're thinking of deploying your talented wife's skills, DON'T!" he shouted the last word and David jumped back in his seat.

The room looked around at them, but Nathan didn't appear to care. He was in charge. He was in charge everywhere he went. "Because if you do," he hissed. "I will take any measure; *a n y   m e a s u r e* necessary to stop her."

Leaving David in a puddle of his own creation, Nathan flashed the smile for one last time before rising to leave. "Goodbye, David. I hope, for your sake, we don't ever meet again."

David nodded.

Today, when they told him Jimmy and Sara were waiting for him, he panicked. How could he tell them he wasn't planning to defend himself; that he had no choice? They'd say "We'll take the risk. We can't let the authorities bully us." But they are naïve. That's exactly what they have to do because the authorities have all the power.

David knew he wasn't a strong man when it came to fighting for his rights, but he was strong when it came to sacrificing himself for those he loved. He hadn't killed Mari; he hadn't even seen her. Protesting his innocence had to be his focus, and who knows. There only had to be *reasonable doubt*. And juries weren't stupid. Reasonable doubt. That was his hope now.

And if it wasn't enough? Well, whatever happened, he wouldn't be mentioning Bigfoot ever again. Family came first.

Chapter Twenty-one

"**N**ervous?"

Jimmy nodded. "Yes, but I really appreciate all you've done, Sara. I literally couldn't attempt to go without you."

Sara beamed. Leaning up on tip-toe, she planted a kiss on her uncle's cheek. "Glad to help. I'm good at organising."

"And hopefully, I'll be good at finding your mum and getting this sorted."

"I wish I was coming," Marcus smiled. "An African adventure sounds amazing." He pouted. "Instead, I've got to go to Gran and Granddad's. They haven't even got good internet!"

"Yeah, and they also haven't got an eight-foot murderous monster living near their house, either!" Sara sneered.

"Sorry, Marcus. I know Sara could cope looking after everything, but they insisted. You know what they're like. And it's too dangerous here."

"It'll be great, little bro. You love the horses and everything."

"Yeah, course."

Another toot from the taxi's horn turned all eyes to the door.

"How have we paid for all this? I mean, a taxi and everything?"

Sara grinned. "Dad's credit card details are stored on my computer from a while back. He can hardly complain, can he!" The three chuckled.

"My mum and dad will be here any minute to pick you up," Jimmy reminded, his hand on the door handle.

"We know. Thanks."

"I'm just saying, you know... Stay safe."

Sara smiled. "We will. You too. Good luck, Uncle Jimmy."

"Yeah. Good luck," Marcus chimed in.

Standing on the doorstep until the taxi left Pen Yr Cwm and Jimmy was out of sight, they went back inside and closed the door. Suddenly alone they felt like the children they were. Seeing the moistness in her brother's eyes, Sara sucked in her own fears and hauled him close for a hug. "It'll be okay. Mum will sort it out. You'll see."

The enormity of responsibility seized Jimmy's chest as soon as the car left his brother's road. Shit. How was he going to do this? He had the contact details. Sara had even arranged for him to be met at the airport by Monique's guide in Congo: a very friendly-sounding native called Awax. They'd spoken on the phone and

Awax told him it would take a while to track down his sister-in-law, but they knew where she had headed.

It would be dangerous. Or maybe risky was more the word. The jungle had its own risks: poisonous snakes, insects and arachnids, mosquitos, even killer plants. They were all a risk. But the danger came from the warring factions who might, at any time, decide to kidnap him, or kill him, or both.

His hand shot to a bead of sweat that made him jump as it dropped from his brow to his cheek. He couldn't do this. He should turn around. *"What else are you going to do?"* Sara's words echoed around his head. What else could he do? He had no choice. If this was the last thing he ever did, it would at least be valiant.

And which was preferable? A long worthless life, or a short heroic one. He shrugged. And there was always the chance he'd survive without being kidnapped or murdered and then he could have both!

He became aware of the drone of the radio interrupting his thoughts...

"So now the Beast of Benfro seems to have done a disappearing act, Pembrokeshire's claiming more paranormal phenomenon! We've had literally dozens of calls from listeners swearing they've seen mysterious bright lights above Caldey Island. Oooh, UFO's now! What a place..."

"Can you turn this off?" Jimmy groaned. He could tell it was with reluctance that his request was upheld, but

Jimmy had to believe in what he was undertaking. He couldn't allow preposterous stories of UFO's to make him disbelieve what was already difficult to cope with. No. He had to stay focussed

He needed a drink. As soon as the taxi pulled into the rank outside Cardiff International Airport and he checked in, Jimmy hurried to Duty-Free and downed half a dozen beers and chasers. By the time his flight was called he was relieved to feel quite numb.

"Welcome to British Airways flight 459 to Paris. We will be arriving at our destination on time at 16:49 local time…"

The first stop was causing enough anxiety. His French was abysmal so connecting with Air France to Kinshasa was not something he felt confident in. There would be no uber-tanned rep signing him up for inebriated excursions before he'd boarded the plane. This was all a bit too grown-up.

Shuffling through the airport waiting to reclaim his bags, he stopped at the bar and struggled, via use of slow speech and made up sign-language, to get a drink. He downed it and then another, and then another.

Checking his bags in for the next leg of his journey was taken care of by patient Parisian airport staff who had dealt with enough drunk Brits to do so politely, albeit with shared looks of disdain with their colleagues.

When he'd fastened his seatbelt and listened to the announcements for flight information (which were luckily repeated in English), for the first time the reality of what he was about to do hit him between the eyes. His hands shook. "Can... Can I get a drink, er, S'il vous plaît?"

"Yes. Of course," the silky French accent lulled him. Monique must have been in her element on her flight.

On this leg of the journey he would have to navigate the airport and transfer to an overnight stay in a hotel by himself. Sara had arranged the accommodation (and paid in advance with his brother's credit card), but he still had to find a taxi. And like Paris, and on the plane, French was the dominant language (although there seemed less resistance to accommodating his terrible attempts, and more willingness to converse in pigeon-English.)

He collected his bags and made his way to the taxi-rank outside. Sleep beckoned, or rather, insisted, and he arrived at his hotel with a shake from his driver.

Before nodding off, he realised, Kinshasa was not what he expected from the capital city. He didn't like to admit what he had envisaged, but the modern tall buildings and wide streets were not it.

And looking up now at the grand hotel he was to spend the night in before heading back to the airport to fly to Bunia tomorrow, he was impressed. This Congo experience was a lot more cosmopolitan than he had feared.

The driver kindly carried Jimmy's bag to the door of the hotel, then spoke in a rapid language Jimmy was sure was not French to a porter who almost disappeared in the night but for the whites of his eyes and tombstone teeth.

"You are very late, Mr Webb. But do not worry. We are expecting you."

The driver glared at Jimmy and didn't move from the door.

"Have you paid for your Taxi, Mr Webb?"

Jimmy flushed red. "Oh sorry!"

As he fished around in his bag for his wallet, the burly porter added, "I suggest you give a generous tip. This is a long way from the airport."

Jimmy held out the wad of Congolese Francs and shrugged. He trusted the porter to hand over the right amount, but thirty-five thousand did seem a lot! The taxi driver looked pleased, but not thrilled as he headed to his car. Jimmy followed the porter to the marble desk where he plucked a key from a hook.

"Follow me," he smiled. Pressing one of the top buttons in the lift, they came to a gliding halt at floor twelve and Jimmy scurried behind along a plush modern corridor.

Throwing open the door to reveal a large room, the porter proceeded to demonstrate the whereabouts of the bathroom, window seating area, writing desk, and television (Jimmy was sure he could have deciphered all these things with his eyes.) He gained Jimmy's full attention when he pointed out the amply filled mini-bar.

Keen to get started, he waited for the man to leave, but he hung around. After attempting to gain Jimmy's cooperation with a cough or two, he was forced to ask. "It is customary, sir, to tip the staff here."

"Oh. Of course." Flicking open his wallet, he looked aghast at the notes. Taking out a five, he knew that was going to be pence, but he didn't want to hand over more than he needed to. He wasn't sure how long it would need to last.

Leaning forward, the porter smiled. "May I?" Plucking a one-thousand Congolese Franc bill from its cramped confines, he arched his eyebrows to ascertain approval. Jimmy nodded gratefully, sure he'd been let off lightly. "Call 01 on the telephone if you need anything," he bowed his head.

Patting the min-bar cabinet, Jimmy grinned back. "I think I'll be okay, thanks."

Jimmy cracked open three beers before he'd even sat down. Sipping the third allowed a new appreciation for the view. The room overlooked a bustling lit street that seemed more suited to America or Japan than what he'd expected here. He smiled to himself as he took a sip. This wasn't so bad. Not so bad at all.

Annoyingly, he was sure he wouldn't sleep now. Oh well. He could catch up on the two-thousand mile internal flight tomorrow.

Chapter Twenty-two

"**W**hat on earth has been happening, Sara?"

Uncle Jimmy clearly hadn't filled her grandparents in on why they needed to stay with them, which was ridiculous. When Sara outlined a brief explanation of their eldest son's predicament (minus Bigfoot) they looked grey. "Oh my goodness. Why didn't someone tell us?"

Sara smiled. "Sorry, Gran. I assumed Dad or Uncle Jimmy had. It has been hectic here, and now Jimmy has gone to find Mum."

"Find her? Is she lost?"

"No, Grandad," joined in Marcus. "She's just away from a phone or her computer doing a photo-shoot, that's all."

His granddad nodded. "I see. Well, she should be here."

Easing into the back of the farm-dirty estate car, Marcus sniffed the air and retched.

"Sorry. You'll have to move those, David and Jimmy's mum indicated some leather straps that Marcus supposed had something to do with horses.

"Er, okay."

"I'll just throw your bag in the boot, okay?"

"Don't throw it, Grandad, it's got my games console in there!" But it was too late.

"Get back, you two," he ordered his beloved Border Collies. "Right. Let's get you to Gran and Granddad's, shall we?" With an unnecessary toot-toot, he spun the wheels on the shingle drive and roared from the valley.

Heading north, they whizzed through the rugged landscape. An hour later, over mountain and river, they arrived in the unpronounceable Llanychaer, and soon FFerm Golygfa FFynon. Sara knew what it meant in English from countless childhood visits. Waterfall view Farm, or literally 'fountain viewpoint farm' and the village was Castle Church or parish. She'd impressed them at school with that when it emerged from her very limited Welsh vocabulary.

It was staying at their grandparents' farm that had led David and Monique to move to the county. They'd fallen in love with the place. They'd decided on the south of the county in the end for its greater access to the M4 Motorway and Cardiff International Airport which Monique used frequently.

Marcus liked it here for a day. Sometimes it was even nice to be away from technology and enjoy the countryside. But with an indeterminate length of stay, he wasn't looking forward to the extra-long school run. And as far as the World Wide Web was concerned, they might as well be in the Bili forest of Democratic Republic of the Congo with their mother and the Apes.

Sara looked longingly at her phone for the last time before they pulled into the driveway, but it was too late. There already was no service.

"Done a disappearing act, has it!" Glyn shook his head as he jumped from his quad to collect the third sheep carcass off the hillside that week. At least the cows were safe in the cowshed. "Well, we've got some bloody big dogs need controlling then. Dew dew, I'll lose the lot at this rate." But he wouldn't. He had a plan. And as he pulled the bag from the back rack and eased the pop-up poles onto the floor, his lips curled. "I'll sort it out myself, as per bloody usual."

The camouflage pattern might not have been the perfect blend for farmland on the Preseli foothills in Llanycefn, but whatever had killed his sheep wouldn't notice in the dark. He was probably wasting his time anyway. It likely had moved on somewhere else by now, but if it did turn up to trouble his livestock again, rare exotic panther or not, it would get both barrels of his shotgun.

He hadn't told anyone where he was heading. He needed Susan rested for the morning's lambing. He couldn't have her worrying about her husband facing a big cat. A few of the mothers hadn't dropped their lambs yet and he had to get this under control before they did. Newborn lambs would be picked off first.

Securing the final guy rope, Glyn pulled up the zip with a satisfying '*zzzzzzz*' and carried his seat inside. It fully reclined but he had no intention of sleeping. Alert from necessity until completing the deed, he would head home afterwards for a rest in his own comfy bed. There was no point giving in to tiredness before then and reclining to 'rest his eyes.'

Yanking his chair foreword, then from side to side, he leaned back and forth and raised his neck up and down. Who designed these stupid hides? The viewing panel was too low to use standing unless you were a dwarf, and sitting was of course too low down. What the intended perch was remained a mystery to Glyn. Opting for a mix of standing slouched over for a time, and then balancing straight-backed on the edge of the seat, he blew through flaring nostrils. "Well, I hope the bastard shows up soon," he muttered.

Stroking the barrels of his gun, he squinted through the viewing slit alternating between stood up and sitting until the dusk light failed and he decided to go outside to use his infra-red scope.

With a firm grip he pulled the zip slowly this time, each '*z*' echoing through the night silence like a buzz saw. Holding his breath and tip-toing out, he moved metres from the tent and brought up the eyepiece. It was harder than he expected to make out anything in the poor light. As he pointed at his flock and counted them off in his head, he laughed to himself that it might send him to sleep. The chuckles were short-lived because he was sure he detected movement.

Heart leaping to his throat, he screwed his eye to the lens and held his breath as though the noise of his own oxygenation might stop him seeing. Eyes bulging in disbelief, he was sure now; it was! It bloody was. Something that wasn't a sheep in the copse of trees at the bottom of the field. Definitely not a sheep, but not a panther either. Was it a hiker? Had his flock been decimated by a person? They'd have to be a sick bastard to dismember his sheep that way. Maybe he should still shoot them! Frowning, he shook his head; big too. Bloody big. What was it?

Grabbing his gun, he jerked it to his shoulder and cocked both barrels. Eye to the lens, he couldn't see without the infra-red. Where was the moon when you needed it? Damned clouds. His torch was bright but would alert whoever, or whatever, was stalking his sheep so he would need to spot it and make a quick decision whether to shoot. Heart thumping, he switched it on and fixed the beam where he'd seen the figure. Nothing. Just trees. "Come on. Where are you?"

The question was answered too fast, but not in a way that made sense to his bewildered mind, and so he spent too long wondering what lumbered towards him and not enough lining up his shot.

Adrenaline surged to save him and he acted on instinct. It was fast. He couldn't outrun it. Would a shotgun kill it, or wound it enough to make a significant impact? Neck rocking back, his eyes sunk into their sockets attempting to hide from the approaching horror. It had to be a thousand pounds, or bigger, didn't it?

The moment of calculation passed and for better or worse, he had no choice but to pull the trigger.

The explosion cracked the sky and the howl that followed said he'd hit his mark. Squeezing his finger to let the second barrel project its deadly shot even closer, it was too late. Long arms swatted the weapon from his grasp so violently his thumb snapped just before his arm ripped from his sleeve.

The spray of lead missed the monster snarling down at him, instead ripping the side of his face and his eye away in a crimson fountain. Unimaginable agony left him praying death would claim him soon as the huge muzzle, creased with fury, snarled down at him, yellowed teeth wet with saliva glinting in the torchlight.

If the dark angel listened, it granted swift mercy as the massive fist of the beast crushed into his chest stopping his heart with the first hit. As his head tore from his neck and bounced along the ground, he was already dead.

Claws tearing at his attacker, the sasquatch pulverised the broken body on the floor before heaving him up and sinking huge canines into his fleshy stomach. Shaking his head from side to side, ribs splitting sent shards of sharp bone into the kidney and through the heart and lungs.

Screeching again, the creature hurled the blood-soaked body to the floor and thumped its mighty chest.

Ginger fingers prodded the punctures on its shoulders where dozens of tiny cuts smarted, hurting more as he touched them. Head back to the wind, it sniffed the air and roared. Feet thumping, it limped away to deal with its wounds in peace.

"What's that?" Karen patted Graham's arm to wake him, but his eyes were already so wide his eyeballs were in danger of tumbling onto the groundsheet of their tent.

"It must be a farmer shooting, I suppose. Rabbits, foxes, I don't know."

"Rabbits! Didn't you hear the noise after the shots?"

Graham nodded in the dark. He had heard. His brain was desperate to generate an innocent explanation. Until he could, the cosy canvas they had erected joyfully hours before felt like woeful protection. "Foxes make some awful noises. And deer!" he leapt on the possibility. "I saw a documentary about red deer in the Scottish Highlands and the stags really growled!"

"But we're in Wales, not Scotland."

"I know, my love," Graham's caustic sarcasm fell on deaf ears as his trembling lips failed to convey his afront. "But deer are common all over Britain aren't they. I'm sure they even farm them around here. It could have been a poacher. Yeah, that makes sense. That's why there were only the two shots."

"Well get out there and look, will you? I won't sleep until I know."

Look? Look for what? What did it matter, and what she expected him to do about it with his Swiss Army knife, he didn't know. But she'd annoyed him now. He'd rather be out of the tent alert to a threat than pretending to sleep whilst doing anything but, terrified and trapped in his sleeping bag.

Breath released in short controlled bursts, he opened the zip silently and crept outside. Standing to his full height, he stretched his well-muscled arms behind his back and grinned. It was flattering how she expected him to be invincible in any situation. The longer he stood, the more convinced he became that if he saw anything it would definitely be a poacher dragging a deer. The notion to scare him grew; make him worry he'd be in trouble. Well he should be.

Padding away from the tent and towards where he thought the noise had come from, he side-stepped twigs before slipping through a gap in the foliage and hiding in a hedge, holding his breath.

He could hear something and it sounded big and lumbering. A giggle played on his lips as it approached. He'd jump out and demand an explanation. Whoever it was would get the surprise of their lives. There would probably be a reward from the farmer. And well-deserved too. Not everyone would be so brave.

The shuffling sound grew closer. A moment of doubt that he risked being shot fell away under the light of logic that he wouldn't have bothered re-loading his gun after making a successful hunt. Bending his knees, he crouched down and when his ears judged the moment to be just right, he leapt from his hiding place. "Holy shit!" he cried instead of the 'What do you think you're doing?' he had planned. Legs struggling to obey his terrified need to flee, fear coaxed them into wobbly action and propelled him scuttling in retreat.

The thuds behind him grew louder but he had to make it back to the tent. Then what? What was he doing? The thought that leading this monster to his wife was a mistake surfaced too late.

His frantic footsteps alerted her to yank open the zipper to check on him just in time to witness his crewcut head leaving his body as two black claw fingers prodded into holes where his eyes had been moments before. The opposite hand gripped Graham's shoulder and tore his neck like a meaty snack.

Warm blood splattered onto her face turning her screams into gargled yelps.

The sound drew the monster's gaze. Throwing the headless corpse of her husband aside like a doll, huge claws thrashed. If she survived, she would look back and laugh at her attempts to stop him with the zip as she tugged it down. But survival wasn't likely.

Pulling the sleeping bag up to her nose, her eyes peeped over the top and she wished she could stop screaming. Flung to the roof of the tent as it flew from the ground, her skull cracked against a tree branch as their cosy camp crashed down metres away.

Clutching her head, she lay silent at last. Screams giving up. There was nothing they could do.

A hair-covered fist plunged through the teeth of the zipper and grabbed sightlessly around the tent. The multi-tool knife Graham was so proud of lay on the floor, dislodged from its place in the pocket on the side of the canvas as it was hurled from its pitch. Pick-picking the blade from its folded slot, with trembling fingers, seemed impossible, but she managed; and as the hand came near, she swung the tiny penknife, thrusting the blunt blade into the monster's flesh with all her strength.

As it clenched its fist, blood squeezed from the wound like an erupting volcano. But the threat in that one bloodied paw told her she'd made a terrible mistake.

The canvas ripped and she had nowhere to hide. Shuffling back, away from its reach, it was toying with her; a mouse to a cruel cat. He can't have been in the mood for much fun, she mused, because it watched her wriggle for only the shortest time before swinging a huge arm and knocking her last breath from her chest.

In her dying moments, highlights flashed before her: her wedding day, Graham running the marathon; Graham competing in Iron Man Wales, which was how they'd discovered Pembrokeshire in the first place leading them to come wild camping in the woods. Her entire adult life had been lived supporting him, and now her last conscious thoughts threatened to be about him too.

Well, screw you, Graham! If we'd gone to IKEA and bought a kitchen like I wanted this weekend, we'd still be alive. For a final thought, it was as good as any, she considered as her throat tore apart in the grip of the beast's mighty claws and her warm blood relinquished the last of her lifeforce into the waiting mouth.

Jimmy slept; against his prediction. He slept so long, that had the hotel not required his room, he would have missed his plane. Rushing with his meagre luggage to reception, he paid his bill on the pre-saved credit-card details of his brother. The thousands and thousands of Congolese Francs meant nothing to his fuggy head. Aware of their low value, it still seemed a fortune. A pang of guilt threatened to dislodge last-night's liquid dinner as he acknowledged a big chunk of the bill came from the empty mini-bar.

The porter from the night before jumbled him into a taxi with a smile and a "Bon voyage," and when he returned to the airport he even remembered to tip. From the grin the cabbie drove away with, Jimmy had overdone it.

Once he checked in his bag, paid his $50 departure tax (Sara had warned him about it but it still came as a shock) with his card, he was soon through to departures. Then he noticed the shaking. Holding his hand out in front of him, his fingers trembled. Forcing his arm down to his side, he stuffed his hands in his pockets.

Entering a large domed room that served as the waiting area, Jimmy was dismayed not to see any facilities. Behind a barrier, a few shops were dotted here and there, but how to get to them was unclear, and he wasn't convinced they'd sell what he needed anyway. It was a far cry from the Duty-Free at Heathrow.

His pasty paleness stood him out against the crowd, but eyes he met greeted with a smile. A family travelling home to Bunia, who had visited the capital for medical care, noticed his taut face and promised to let him know when the flight was due to board. He clutched his documents including his pink receipt for departure tax, without which he wouldn't be allowed to board.

Good to their word, they gave him the nudge and he joined the throng for the plane

A lager on the flight took the edge off his nerves. The savannah scenery below, incredible in its vastness, gave him an agoraphobic nausea.

As the aeroplane banked north-east, the grassland gave way to forest. Hundreds upon hundreds of miles of deep dark jungle. Jimmy was convinced that there could be any number of undiscovered creatures living there.

The two-thousand mile journey terminated some four and a half hours later as the plane touched down in what was essentially a field. Exiting via steep steps, the humidity hit like a hot towel. Threatening clouds above jostled to be the first to pour their burden on the forest below. Jimmy nodded to himself feeling lucky to have arrived safely.

The terminal was a simple white rectangle. The corrugated roof looked to be asbestos. Oh well. Add it to the list of things that might attempt to kill him. Despite its smallness, the building contrived to take up a lot of his time. He felt like a criminal as he was probed regarding his reasons for travel. His boozy breath probably didn't help.

Eventually, he stumbled into the daylight, darkening in with ever-angrier storm clouds. With the first vicious rumble, he heard his name.

"Mr Jimmy? I am Awax, we spoke on the telephone. I've been expecting you." A big smile and a firm grip of a dark hand welcomed him "How was your flight? Good, I hope."

English, spoken perfectly. Why was it, shanty towns in the deepest jungle spoke half-a-dozen languages, yet all his friends struggled with the intricacies of their native tongue?

"Come. I have a car. We will go to the city and get you some food, yes?"

Jimmy nodded. The city? He didn't remember seeing a city from the air. Hurrying from the terminal building to beat the rain, Jimmy saw a number of cars; none of which looked like he wanted to get in them. MOT certificates were obviously not a requirement in Democratic Republic of the Congo.

"Here we are." Awax stopped at a relatively robust looking four-by-four with most of the usual features in about the right place. The dents gave it character. It had led an adventurous life. "Put your bag in the back."

As the rain hit, Jimmy could barely see through the windscreen. Caked on dust became mud in the downpour. Awax turned the wipers onto full-blast and carried on.

As they scraped away the grime, Jimmy gazed out, wondering when the cityscape might fill his view. But then he realised, the small number of buildings he'd assumed were part of the airport was it.

Comprising a dusty, now muddy street with dilapidated shops, it was like the Wild-West. There was even a saloon with swing doors. He half-expected John Wayne to stagger out, or perhaps Clint Eastwood throwing his poncho over his shoulder ready to blast him out of town.

People scurried around wrapped in pieces of polythene from packages, or sat under makeshift stalls covered with tarpaulin roofs. Jimmy wondered why they didn't go inside, but as soon as the rain began than it stopped. The sun beat down and everybody discarded their shelters into bags and pockets or even just along the road.

Houses dotted the land around the main thoroughfare. The high-pitch whine of revving motorbikes filled the air above the calls to buy from the street vendors which had risen again after the rain.

Awax pulled the big Shogun into a space outside a building full of rustic charm. There was nothing but space. Jimmy imagined a parking ticket was something they would laugh at here. The atmosphere was one of lawless cooperation.

"Come. There's good food here. It is where Miss Monique stays." He said his sister-in-law's name with a nasty glint of over-appreciation.

Barging through a wooden door that last received paint when Queen Victoria was a girl, Jimmy found himself in a surprisingly well appointed dining room. There were no customers, despite the damp outside, but he could see Monique lapping up its rustic charm.

"Roland. Bring me two of today's specials, s'il vous plaît."

Roland peeped out from a hidden room Jimmy assumed must be the kitchen and grinned. His smile so white in his dark face, Jimmy almost squinted at the contrast.

He didn't speak, but moments later; as if he had expected them and had prepared the meal in advance, he placed plates in front of his guests. Food, a jumble, looked like the scrapings after an Indian meal—rice, leaves, bits of this and that. There was fish too, and when Jimmy allowed himself a taste, the grin bisecting his face was inexorable.

"MMmm. This is good. Tres bien!" Roland grinned, still wordlessly. Jimmy wondered if he was unable to speak.

When the miracle of the delicious food subsided in his head, Jimmy remembered why he was there. Swallowing a full mouthful, he said, "My sister-in-law stayed here, you say, Awax?"

"Yes," Awax nodded between fork-fulls. "We haven't seen her for weeks though."

Jimmy's face dropped. It struck him there must be a lot of places to get lost in three weeks in the Bili forest.

"Why do you want her?"

Jimmy pondered coming straight out with it, but moderated his explanation to keep his credibility. "We may have discovered a new species of primate. We need my sister-in-law to come and track it down. There's a lot riding on it."

Awax nodded. He didn't show the slightest interest; didn't ask what type of primate they were talking about. Instead, he outlined his plan. "I can take you to where she planned to set up camp. She might have moved on, but not too far. She's no fool."

"When do we go?"

"You need your rest. You can have Monique's usual room here. It's nothing much, but it's cheap."

Jimmy winced and opened his wallet. "Take what you need. I'm still clueless, sorry."

Awax jostled a hefty bundle of cash from Jimmy's wallet. Splitting it in two, he held one fistful out, "This for our supplies, okay?"

Jimmy nodded. This really was turning into an adventure, and he had to confess, he was enjoying it.

"We will travel as far as we can by road, but with yesterday's rain, we might not get far. And more rain's expected."

"What will we do then?" Jimmy could feel a jungle hike coming on.

"Your sister-in-law's camp is up river a hundred miles or so."

"Are you sure you can find it?" Jimmy gulped. It seemed so impossible.

Awax laughed. "I took her there. I know where it is."

The Mitsubishi Shogun made it a good way into the jungle and now darkness was setting in. "We'll camp here for the night," Awax announced.

Awax set about building a fire like Bear Grylls on acid. In what seemed like minutes, he had a roaring flame over which he had set up a pot on a hook. "We'll need plenty of clean water for our trip up the river."

The lo-tech four-by-four proved anything but when the luggage on the roof rack was transformed into a two-man tent.

"I assumed we'd set up camp in a clearing on the ground. I guess that's safe, is it?"

Awax smiled and shrugged.

"What, is it not safe?" Jimmy's eyes bulged.

"It's saf*er*. There are a lot of big predators out here, Mr Jimmy. But really, leopards and lions will try to avoid us."

"Leopards? Lions?"

Awax chuckled. "Snakes and spiders are less likely off the ground too, but can fall from the canopy. And wild boar won't bother us up here on the roof. But what we really need to avoid is crocodiles. They aren't wary of man like the big cats, and up here, we are safe from them." Awax rummaged around in his bag and brought out a fishing reel. "Now. You want to help me catch a fish?"

It was nearly dark, and he did not want to stand on the edge of a river infested with crocodiles dangling bait. He didn't want to *be* bait. Maybe that was Awax's plan! Perhaps he wanted crocodile steak for tea.

Shining a torch onto the water, Awax sighed. "There's a croc across the river. You see its eyes?" The glint of two amber sphere's sent a shudder down Jimmy's spine. "We better hope he isn't hungry!"

Striding to the water's edge, Awax beckoned. "Keep the light on him, but look out for movement along the bank. There may be a few."

Jimmy's jelly legs struggled to move him.

"Unless you want me to keep a vigil and you hold the line in the river?"

Jimmy shook his head and trained the shaking beam across the water. The dead eyes stared back.

"If they disappear, you must tell me."

Jimmy nodded.

Despite his anxiety, the time it took for Awax to hook three sizeable fish from the river seemed like seconds. Spearing the catch onto a sturdy twig, he smoked them over the fire. While they cooked, he decanted boiled water into a Gerry can. "We have water, but it is always best to stock up when you have opportunity. Only a fool runs out."

"How do you keep so calm? I mean fishing with a monster that could devour you in one bite metres away?" Jimmy shook his head and then blurted. "We are safe from them here, aren't we?"

"You are never completely safe in the jungle, my friend. You must make calculated risks. Our croc friend wasn't interested when we were on the river bank. It is unlikely he would trouble us now, and we are plenty far back from the edge."

"Then, why do we need to sleep on the roof of the truck?"

Awax squeezed his chin in his fingers. "It is difficult to make a considered risk assessment when you are sleeping. It is important to keep as safe as possible."

"I don't know how you cope. I appreciate you helping me, but I couldn't live like that. Danger around every corner. Why are you laughing?"

Awax controlled himself. "More people die on your roads in a day than would die from croc attacks in Africa in a year. And yet you all live with that; most of you taking that risk every single day without giving the danger the respect it warrants. I never forget the perils of the jungle. Many people are killed by wild animals, of course they are. I may meet my end that way too. But I don't take unnecessary risks so I keep the threat to a minimum."

Colour drained from Jimmy's face. "Thanks, Awax. I'm greatly reassured... not."

Awax chuckled. "The wildlife is not the principal menace here, my friend."

"What do you mean?" Jimmy flinched.

Shifting on his rock seat and looking uncomfortable for the first time, Awax said, "I hope you are fortunate enough never to find out. But these are treacherous times, Mr Jimmy, serious times." Seeing Jimmy's face, he grinned. "Here. This might calm your nerves." Handing Jimmy the biggest roll-up he'd ever seen put him at the top of his all-time heroes list.

"Maybe I can live with the danger after all!"

Chapter Twenty-three

Apart from a moment in the night where Jimmy debated his need for a wee and decided he'd rather wet himself than get off the roof of the Shogun on his own, he had slept well. Awax was already up and putting the finishing touches to a canoe that had been hidden until now.

"Wow, Awax. Where did you hide that?"

"It folds. These planks keep it stable."

"Are you sure we'll be safe on a foldable boat?" Jimmy was alarmed. He'd expected something moored up river. He had no idea they'd brought the craft with them.

"Of course I'm not sure!" Awax snapped.

Jimmy sank against the front grill of the car. "That's not what I wanted to hear."

"Well, I'm sorry I can't dress it up any better for you. But these are dangerous times. And I don't mean the crocs. They are the least of our worries. You can reason with a croc... Predict what it might do. Our neighbours, on the other hand; not so much..."

"Neighbours?"

"Yes, Mr Jimmy. Did you look at a map before coming here? Hey? We are very close to people who hate us and

163

of course, it could be bad. Very bad. You must love your brother."

Filled with a steely determination, Jimmy stood to his full height. "Yes. I do. Come on, let's go."

Jimmy nodded, impressed, when with a single rip of the chord the little outboard buzzed into life immediately. Combined with the modern folding boat, it was all very reassuring. "Awax, this isn't what I expected. I mean, it looks expensive."

Awax smiled. "Five million."

Jimmy laughed. "How much is that in money I can understand?"

"Around about three thousand dollars."

Nodding, Jimmy knew that was a lot more reasonable, but still; that was a considerable sum of money. Expecting his confusion, Awax added, "Your sister-in-law paid plenty for my help, and others before her. I said I needed it and they happily paid. It is for your safety after all."

The guilt he'd felt dragging Awax into the jungle evaporated. He hadn't thought this was his job.

The craft was perfect. Its slick fibre-glass hull leak-free, and the low draught made navigating the murky water easy.

"How long will it take to get to Monique's camp?" Jimmy asked over the noise of the engine.

"Less than a week."

Jimmy thought they'd arrive later on today. He wasn't prepared for nights on end panicking about animal attacks like last night; especially without the safety of the car roof.

"Maybe much less, depending on the rain. If it rains hard, the river will flow against us reducing our speed. If it stays dry, we could halve the time."

"What do you expect?"

"It's hard to tell. We are right in the middle of the rainy season and there will be precipitation every day. It depends how much."

Jimmy slouched in the boat. For the first time, the uncertainty seemed like a nightmare.

Camping on the second night was in a river clearing. Awax strung hammocks between sturdy trees and propped the dinghy up so that it offered a barrier against crocs. He reassured that the further up river they went, the smaller the crocodiles they could expect to encounter. Snakes were now the biggest threat—apart from their human enemies.

There had been no rain that day, despite the season. It seemed perhaps the powers that be were smiling on them.

"We will make it today," Awax beamed. "God willing. It is not that far now. We must pray for dry weather."

Jimmy had no problem with that and immediately clasped his hands together and prayed to all gods he could name.

As the little boat buzzed against the gentle flow of the river, Awax's assurances hung in the air. Every bend in the river looked the same. How could he tell they were close?

As dusk set in, Jimmy knew the score. They had fifteen minutes at most to set up camp. When Awax pulled the boat ashore and disappeared into the jungle, Jimmy wasn't prepared.

Leaves moved and Awax's dark head poked through. "Come along. The camp is this way."

A giggle of glee rippled through his chest. He hadn't known they had arrived. Awax keeping it from him until now struck as typical of his sense of humour.

Jimmy's joy was short-lived when his comrade glared at him and put a finger to his lips. Jimmy's knees weakened. He suddenly imagined himself face to face not with pretty Monique, but fearsome guerrillas, or the infamous lion-eating Bili apes themselves. It was with more than a little relief when the sight which greeted him next was of a tent in a clearing. A light glowed through the fabric.

"Good," Awax whispered. "It looks like they are here. They haven't ventured away from the site."

That would have been a bummer.

A noise from inside stopped Awax dead. Ducking down, he gestured for Jimmy to do the same. Unpleasant crashes of tins and cups echoed from within the tent. Not the professional silence of a famous primatologist in her element.

Crouching, hurt. Easing his right leg out, Jimmy rubbed away the cramp threatening to set into his thigh. Putting all his weight on his bent left leg caused an immediate and excruciating spasm. Jimmy collapsed onto the ground and rubbed vigorously at his leg to beat the convulsion away. Awax stood. Whoever was in the tent couldn't have missed the noise.

Chapter Twenty-four

"**M**onique?" Brad stumbled from the tent, fumbling the flap back in place. He held a rifle to his shoulder and called again, "Monique? Monique, is that you?"

His gaze fell on Jimmy lying on the floor, and then to Awax standing beside him. Squinting, he lowered his rifle. "Awax. What are you doing here? I thought you were Monique."

"Not quite as pretty, though, eh?" Awax stepped forward. Bending in front of Jimmy, he held out two outstretched arms offering to haul him to his feet.

"Who's this?" Brad asked, stumbling forward.

Once on his feet and rubbing his leg with his left hand, he offered his right for Brad to shake. He'd heard from David that he was handsome, but his brother had underplayed how handsome for his own sanity. Brad's piercing blue eyes shone out of a rugged, tanned face, alert beyond its inebriation.

He wore a beaded necklace, similar to several he's seen worn back in Bunia; the angled shark-tooth design pointed down to his open shirt and a set of abs that looked like crocodile skin, and just as tough.

"I'm James Webb. Monique's brother-in-law. Where is Monique?" Jimmy asked, hoping that Brad's drunken state didn't indicate what he feared: that Monique was nowhere close by.

Brad's hand hovered in mid-air before flopping at his side without taking Jimmy's. "What do you want?" he spat, turning back towards the tent.

"It's really important. David's in trouble. I need to take Monique home with me. I know how busy she is here, but she'll want to come back after I tell her why."

Brad flopped in a chair, his face in his hands. Throwing himself back suddenly, Jimmy was surprised to see him laughing.

"What's funny," Jimmy demanded. Awax stood aside. He'd done his part delivering Jimmy to camp.

"Nothing!" Brad stopped laughing and stood. "Nothing at all." Storming from the tent, his drunken stoop from before now barely noticeable; his visitors' presence having had a sobering influence. Brad came to a stop a few feet away and turned once again to face Jimmy and Awax. "You've got to be kidding me, right? Where's bloody Monique?" he snarled.

Jimmy's eyes had sought out the alcohol like a bee to a flower. Appearing at the flap of the tent with the bottle of whiskey and two glasses, he smiled. "Let's have a drink and a chat."

With the glasses shared between Awax and Jimmy, Brad took another swig from the bottle.

"So we had travelled further than planned and came out of the jungle near some little town further west… close to Isiro; Dungo or Dumbo or something." Brad paused and Jimmy nudged him to continue.

"We got some supplies, and Monique checked her phone, the same as she did every fucking day. But this day; this one day, she got like, half a bar of signal and a message from her daughter." Brad took a big swig. "She was going to leave him. We were planning to be together. That's what I thought, anyway."

Jimmy put his glass on the table. A significant gesture of disapproval against the man responsible for much of his brother's distress. "Where is she now?" Jimmy demanded, ready to ram the bottle into Brad's smarmy face if he didn't stop with the self-pity and start telling them what they needed to know.

"She's gone… Hitched a ride to Isero to get on a plane there. She must be back in the U.K. by now."

Colour drained from Jimmy. All this time and Monique had been heading home anyway! There was no reason for him to stay. His mission was already accomplished. He began to laugh. "Well, she didn't take much persuasion, then!" he grabbed the bottle from Brad's firm grip and poured a big glass full of the amber fire. "How soon can we head back? Monique will need to be put in the picture. And it's not safe at home." His words faded as he looked around him at the perilous surroundings she'd survived for weeks.

Answering the raised eyebrows, Jimmy decided to tell. "We've got our own mysterious primate in Pleasant Valley."

Brad's eyes opened wide. "What do you mean?"

"David saw what he's describing as a bigfoot in the woods near his house. And a woman's dead!"

"Bigfoot? Don't be so stupid!" Brad yelled.

"What, you don't believe in them?"

"That's not the point. There's every chance there could be undiscovered apes matching the description, but not in bloody Wales! It's only the size of a football field!"

"I know. It seems crazy, but we heard it. I got that telly program *Seeking Sasquatch* to come and investigate."

Brad's eyes opened even wider. "Jeez. What did they say?"

"*They* said they were certain they'd heard a sasquatch, but their schedule wouldn't allow them to stick around and get proof. That's why we need Monique home. She'll find it, won't she?"

Brad sat forward on his chair. "And would her daughter…"

"Sara."

"… Sara. Yeah. I know." Brad glared. "Would she have mentioned all this in her message?"

Jimmy shrugged. "I presume so. We wanted Monique to hurry home. I can't see her leaving out anything important that might persuade her."

Brad stood again. Pacing back and forth in the tiny space. "It makes sense now. Of course. She doesn't care about David! She wants to keep this discovery to herself. Good ol' Brad's fine to risk his life in the bloody Congo, but in super-safe Wale's, he's not needed."

Jimmy hated hearing him talk in the third person. "Whatever, it doesn't sound like she wants to be with you, does it?"

"Scheming little bitch."

"Hey!" Jimmy objected. Squaring up had no effect.

Brad squeezed contempt from slit eyes as he looked Jimmy's slight frame up and down.

In desperation, Jimmy threw a punch to Brad's granite chin. Despite starting out drunk and having almost drained the last of the bottle, Brad side-stepped the clumsy attack with ease. In, return, he threw his own square fist forward and ploughed it hard into Jimmy's soft face.

With the thud of leather on willow, Jimmy's nose exploded in a sickening crunch. Blood splattered down his shirt and up the sides of the tent. "No!" Awax screamed, flinching from the spray on his skin.

Buoyed by his effect, Brad brought his other fist in hard to the side of Jimmy's skull.

Eyeballs rolling in the back of his head, Jimmy fell to the floor; eyelids flapping shut was the last thing he remembered.

Chapter Twenty-five

Monique had touched down at Cardiff airport and phoned Sara the second she got off the plane. Along with the answerphone recording came the dozen or more messages Sara had left her. They had become ever-decreasing in information and ever-increasing in severity. Whatever the truth, it had certainly rattled her staid and sensible daughter.

When she arrived to an empty house, she knew what she had to do. If David needed a bigfoot to prove his innocence, then she wasn't going to rest until she found it.

Rummaging in her desk, she pulled the Ordnance Survey map from within a pile of papers. Spreading it out on the table she studied with a keen eye. She decided it best to assume there was something in the woods. She didn't have time for 'ifs' and 'maybes.' If it was good enough for Sara, and good enough for her husband, it was good enough for her.

So, where could an eight-foot sasquatch hide in Pleasant Valley? David apparently saw the creature in the woods. Sara described him seeing it across the valley when walking Jess. It depends on the animal's intelligence, she pondered.

The apes she'd encountered in the Bili forest were clever. They lived in an organised hierarchical society. But they didn't actively avoid human contact; more their habitat is so hidden they have only been seen recently because of that.

That's what Monique had always assumed was the case with the sasquatch and yeti. And given territory as vast as North America or the Himalaya, that assumption seemed fair. But if a creature that large lived in the limited environment of Pembrokeshire, then there was no doubt: it had to be deliberately keeping out of sight.

But it must sleep somewhere. It must have a place it disposes of or hides the bones of its prey, or evidence would have been uncovered long ago.

Tapping a bronzed finger against full pink lips, she studied the map. She had barely seen the locality. Since they'd moved in after falling in love with the county on visits to David's parents, she had been away as long as she'd been home.

But fresh eyes could be an advantage. She had a track record of finding animals when others had struggled. Admittedly, that had been with the help of Brad, but she was sure she didn't need him. She couldn't be doing with him since he'd behaved so unprofessionally in Africa, anyway.

She'd flirted, of course. It was her nature. But only because she trusted him and thought he realised she loved her husband.

On occasion, she had to admit to being tempted; he was incredible to look at, but temptation meant nothing. Now she was here to find Bigfoot and save the day.

Her mind had wandered, but her eyes in soft focus had taken it all in. Caves featured everywhere on the Preseli Mountains, carved out by water, but more than that, there were man-made caverns and tunnels in the form of mines; labelled and numerous. Most were inaccessible, some were visited frequently, but one interested her more than any other.

With easy access to fields where a beast could prey on farm animals, hares and rabbits, and woodland where it would find deer, the proximity to where David witnessed it made it the most obvious choice.

And the fact it appeared on private property and was labelled *'Danger-Keep out!'* confirmed it. That's where she would look; and when Monique Xerri had a hunch, it was usually correct.

She was tired. The flight from Isiro to Kinshasa had been hard, and from there to Paris, shattering. Departure times, combined with exhaustion, had meant an overnight stay. So now, back in Wales, she was feeling the value.

She'd never be able to sleep. Not with something so monumental on her doorstep. So, checking her camera had sufficient battery for a night-time vigil, she was ready; but for one other thing to take.

Opening the door to the garage, she steered through the debris of long-dumped junk. As she moved the stepladder, a box she hadn't realised was leaning on it for support gave up and threw itself to the floor, puking its miscellaneous contents in an untidy heap. "Why have we even got half of this rubbish?" Monique kicked the pile, moving the bulk, then ploughed through the rest with the ladder's legs, muttering the while.

Propping the stepladder against the joists which ran the length of the room, she extended her arm to rummage in the overhead storage in the ceiling. Looking down, she scowled; it would take a lot of re-organising before a car could ever fit in here. And the home gymnasium they'd tentatively planned was never going to happen, was it?

Feeling for a brown faux-leather bag between long-discarded junk, she tutted to herself. Where was it? Dismayed, she walked back into the kitchen and smiled to see what she was looking for right there in its carrier near the coat rack.

The smile was short lived as the gun's presence demonstrated how terrified her poor children must have been. And what use would an air-rifle be against an eight-foot ape?

Prizing the rifle from its snug fit, a little shake freed it from the bag. She checked the rifled barrel. It was a nice looking weapon. A glance down the telescopic lens reminded her of its night-vision capabilities. Her camera had that, of course, but if she needed to defend herself, clear sight from the other side of the gun might prove invaluable.

Stroking the muzzle, she recalled when they'd first moved in and bought it to kill the rat that would run along the wall every morning. David had been horrified and had set up camp in the back door to shoot it. The rat must have known, because it never showed up again. The 2.2mm air-rifle had languished in the garage ever since.

"You don't even know if it would have killed that rat, and now you're going to defend yourself against a giant!" Shaking her head, she slung it over her shoulder. Maybe she could scare it at least. Gulping, she chewed at a fingernail. This was a bad idea; but she couldn't wait.

With her camera around her neck, her torch in her hand and the rifle on her back, Monique Xerri, intrepid explorer of the four corners of the globe, took a deep breath and stepped from her front door onto the shingle drive. Squinting up at the sky, she forced her foot forward. She could do this.

The map folded into her jacket pocket wouldn't be needed. Monique knew where she was headed. There was only one place a sasquatch could hide.

Heart pounding in her head, Monique walked up the hill past H's house. No lights shone from within, but Monique kept her torch off and scurried past. Why? What was a septuagenarian farmer going to do? He was doubtless tucked up full of cocoa hours ago.

Bracing against the night air, Monique finally reached a sturdy gate: *Danger! Keep Out. Old Mine* With a gulp, she gripped the top bar and hauled her leg over. Dropping to the other side, she touched her palms to the floor. Standing straight, she dusted herself on her trousers and shone her torch around her.

Chapter Twenty-six

"So, if Monique's already gone back to Wales, there's no bloody point me being here, is there," Jimmy whined through his swollen nose as he dabbed at it with a wet cloth which Brad had passed him to appease his guilt.

"No. And I am not going to let her leave me on the sidelines while she uncovers one of the great mysteries of our time, mate."

Jimmy wasn't sure why Brad's attitude towards his sister-in-law affronted him so. She had always treated him with contempt. But the pain in his undoubtedly broken nose made sure he suffered in silence.

Awax smiled at the easy money. One night at camp before heading straight back was considerably less than he'd anticipated. Glancing around the tent, he wondered where they would all sleep tonight. Squinting his eyes, he edged towards the bed, and while Mr Jimmy sat snuffling, and GI Joe paced the room, he claimed his space on the mattress.

Jimmy woke to heated shouting outside. The canvas directors chair he'd fallen asleep in creaked as he shifted to hear better. He couldn't understand a word, but he could tell they were angry.

Focussing his squint around the inside of the tent, he saw Awax was missing. His space on the bed filled by Brad and the tent was empty.

Lying on top of the sheets, shirt unbuttoned, presenting his sculpted abs to the morning, Brad let out a carefree snore as he commandeered the bed with his starfish position. Awax must have vacated feeling awkward.

With shocking momentum, the tent flaps flew open and a number of loud men stormed inside. "Je Jingo. Jingo! Gue!" screamed a very dark man in military attire. Pointing an automatic rifle at Jimmy, he repeated the command before spotting Action Man on the bed and shouting similar incomprehensible loathing at him.

"Jingo, jingo!" he snarled.

Jimmy's swaying limbs struggled to keep him upright as he feebly thrust his hands to his head as he expected was what the man commanded. A fist jabbed his back and he winced from a vicious shove into the dark of first light. From the corner of his eye, he shuddered as Brad was dragged from the bed to the floor with merciless aggression. His first waking sight would be the menacing muzzle of a machine gun.

Outside, Awax stood defiant, legs apart, hands on head, the steely determination glinting in his eye told him apart from his pasty comrade. Guns all around were trained on him from a group of ten or more soldiers in army uniform.

180

Inches from his face, a gangling giant snarled, saliva spraying in his fury over his captive's skin.

Brad landed at Jimmy's feet before being yanked to standing by his hair. Opening his mouth, he spoke to their captors in their own language.

Jimmy could only stare as Brad and Awax attempted a calm explanation in the face of the aggression, unable to understand a word. It wasn't clear if it had worked: they hadn't been shot, and considering the hostility they demonstrated, that seemed reason to be thankful.

From behind, another fierce prod headed Jimmy away from the tent. A glance sideways showed Brad and Awax getting the same treatment. As they were escorted from their camp, they knew this could not be good.

The path through the jungle had been cleared by their captors on their way in, aiding now, their rapid progress to a clearing a mile away. As they stepped from the dense jungle into the light of day, they could see military vehicles standing. Waiting.

Jimmy cringed at Awax's head bouncing off the side of one of the trucks as two of the men slung him inside. When he was led to yet another vehicle, it was clear: they weren't going to be allowed to talk.

There was barely room to breathe as he was bent onto a bench seat in the back of the waggon. Flanked by two burly guards, another sat opposite, his gun pointing at Jimmy's chest the entire way ensured he would remain on his very best behaviour.

Making eye-contact inadvertently whilst looking out of the back flap of the waggon, Jimmy winced at a sharp dig with the butt of a rifle. The rest of the way, he stared at the floor while the truck bumped over a dirt track for what must have been two hours or more.

Occasional hidden glances showed they had come out of the forest into a mountainous clearing in the full afternoon sun. Another hour passed and they arrived at some makeshift buildings, one of which was evidently their destination because the trucks pulled to a dusty halt outside.

Squinting at the dropping sun, he saw a long, single-story building with a corrugated roof. Without seeing his companions, Jimmy was hauled from the back of the truck and jostled through two doors. As they swung shut, the men hollered in their foreign language to people inside.

Jimmy counted five doors leading off a dingy corridor, as he shunted step by step to the end. He would do whatever they wanted without resistance. Why they had to push him everywhere, he had no idea.

Reaching the fifth and final door, one of the men rapped robustly on the flaking wood. No answer came from inside. Raising a booted foot, he pressed it against the door and threw it open with a vicious kick.

Flying back on its hinges, the handle banged the wall. "Gwe," he pointed at a chair behind a small table. When Jimmy shrugged, he grabbed his arm and swung him towards the plastic seat. "Gwe!" he yelled. "Sit," he added with a frown.

Jimmy sat.

Heart pounding, he flinched at the words yelled at him, nodding, desperate to stop them being angry. Eyes red, he sucked back a tear threatening to betray his masculinity.

"Da." Pointing his strong dark finger, he replaced his beret and barked again, "Da!"

Jimmy didn't know what he meant and sat rigid at the table. A relaxing of the pin-prick pupils led Jimmy to believe he was doing the right thing. Perhaps 'da' meant 'stay.'

Confirming the likelihood, the man pointed at his gun before stepping from the room and slamming the door. Through the gap under the splitting wood, Jimmy could see the shadow of his boots. He was still there, guarding the door.

Alone, he forced himself to take in his surroundings. From flecks of paint that hadn't given up, he could tell it had once been green; a revolting shade that put him in mind of a particularly gruesome bowel movement he'd had after a particularly gruesome night out. Now, the paint had faded and flaked to reveal pale plaster beneath.

A window, at a good height to jump from to escape, had been secured with black iron bars. Was this prison? Had they broken local laws? Images of torture pierced his mind and he shuddered. What would happen to him? He knew he wasn't the type to endure suffering. He'd crumble at the first hint of pain. Gulping, he knew he'd squeal *before* any pain if he only knew what they wanted.

The sun continued its arc across the sky. Time went on as it had before, as it would always do; unaware, or uncaring of Jimmy's plight. He was as insignificant as he had always been.

Lazy eyes tried to decide if the soldier's feet still waited outside the door. He wouldn't risk their wrath by leaving the chair to find out. Motionless but for shallow breaths, his body refused him distance from the here and now. It craved attention and began its demands. He needed the toilet. He needed food. And he was afraid.

Another failure. His whole mission had been a waste of time. Whatever Monique was achieving back home, he wasn't a part of it. He wasn't the hero of the hour he'd hoped to be. The only positive he'd scraped from a barrel full of negatives had now succumbed to its fate like every good thing he ever tried to do.

If this was it. If this was how it ended for James Webb... He gulped down a wad of hurt. His hands trembled so much on his lap they made him jump. Oh, for the sound of a ring pull ripping, or a crown cap popping and spinning on the counter.

Staring at the table, he shook his head. When was the last time he'd sat without a beer within reach and a pack of papers ready to roll the magic herb? What would he give to have them now? Just for a minute. Just to escape the downward swirl of his thoughts for a few moments.

He didn't believe he justified being called an alcoholic; more alcohol reliant than dependent. Perhaps, escape reliant might be a better term. Because it wasn't withdrawal he avoided by drinking or smoking weed or whatever else; it was life: specifically his part in it.

His breathing fell shallower. He was barely conscious. Why was he so useless? Opportunities had come, and he'd missed them. Now, here he was, nearly thirty years old with nothing to his name, living on his brother's sofa. And not even wanted.

He'd needed this to be the turning point and return home the hero who saved the day. Maybe, he'd have actually felt welcome for the first time in his life. Now, if he made it out alive, he'd be a bigger burden than ever.

His hands dropped to his sides, their shaking stopping. Even his dependency was giving up. Hunched, motionless, eyes staring, Jimmy awaited his fate.

Chapter Twenty-seven

It was vast, as Monique knew it would be from studying the map. Squinting, it was impossible to make out, but the dark mass in the distance had to be the forest. Unclear from the valley floor, Ordnance Survey showed the woodland linked to Colby and beyond. Unlikely, perhaps, but an intelligent creature could use the cover to travel all around the county unseen.

The question of why it had attacked and killed her neighbour loomed larger with proximity. From this height, the jagged skyline of harvested forest was obvious. Whole swathes of timber had been cut down. Trees that had grown for more than thirty years were now ripe for harvest by the forestry commission who planted them.

Mari had been unlucky. But with her vast knowledge of primate behaviour, Monique felt assured she wouldn't meet the same fate.

Reaching the edge of the woodland, she paused, and, cupping her hands, she prepared to make the call. From her research she knew it sounded like something between a peacock and an Orang-Utan. Wishing she'd had time to practice, she had to let it out anyway and it sounded terrible. Great, she thought, now I don't know if there's no response because the beast is far away, or because the calling was useless.

Sounding it first in her head, when she tried it again she took great care to make it as loud and accurate as she could. Cupping her hands to her mouth, her squeal echoed through the woods and along the valley. That was better. Holding her breath, Monique waited and listened. Nothing.

Shining the torch through the densely planted trees illuminated only a small area and a short distance. As Monique took a step forward, her knee wobbled and she slipped on soft mud underfoot. The beam of light shook in her trembling grip, "Sheet," she hissed in her French accent. "What arre you doing?"

One quivering foot in front of the other, Monique edged through the forest. Everywhere looked the same. How would she ever find what she was looking for? Pulling the map from her pocket, her shaking fists struggled to unfold it to show anything meaningful. Blinking from the torchlight reflecting from the stark paper, she retraced her steps with her fingers. Tapping the route, she was sure where she was. Sureish.

So, if she was correct about her position, the entrance to the mine must be... she stared into the distance and again at the map trying to fix on a datum to walk towards, but there was nothing; just row upon row of dark conifer awaiting their own harvesting, their needles trembling in the hilltop breeze like hair on the back of prey as it senses a nearby hunter. Shrugging, Monique headed off in the direction indicated and hoped the criss-cross of paths would keep her on track.

Striding now, map still in hand, from nowhere a cry stopped her dead. Stunned, she dropped the torch. It hit the ground and bounced a few feet. The cry came again: the call of the sasquatch, just as she'd imagined.

Gulping, she bolted forward and scooped up her torch. Instinctively, she pushed the button and turned it off. Monique forced breaths in and out with repressed control. Where had the sound come from? She couldn't tell. Be careful, she coached. Just a photo would do. A picture proving the existence of a hitherto undiscovered species, and her world could begin to make sense again. "Just stay safe," she drilled. Heaving the air-rifle from her shoulder, she looked through the sights.

Peering through the telescope of the gun gave a much needed sense of detachment. She could see much better than with the torch, was safer than behind her camera, and less obvious too.

Her heart raced. The cry had been close: not feet away, but near enough that a sasquatch running at speed would catch her off guard. She had to stay alert. If it rushed her, she could shoot. It wouldn't do much damage, but might buy her enough time to escape. The watermelons they'd obliterated for practice in the garden could attest to that.

A noise from behind made her jerk as an owl flew close to her head. "Holy sh…" she hissed under her breath. Another sound in front of her shot her round again.

Movement up ahead dropped her to the floor. Peering from hidden safety, she struggled to control her gasping need for air. When she recognised what had drawn her gaze, she let out a sigh of relief: H walking through the woods. What was he doing out so late? Did he ever sleep?

Preparing to stand, the grunt of a large animal stopped her dead.

"That's it. In you go," the soothing tone of a careful owner pierced the veil of night and the approaching dawn. Another grunt and a dragging sound. Monique gasped. Yanking her camera from her neck, she gave it the space the rifle had occupied. 'Snap, click, Snap.'

She had it! She had her picture. Not crisp, but it was unmistakable. Mere metres away, the hulking figure of an unknown ape-like species lumbered towards her neighbour. Behind, it dragged a doe, her head bobbing over the rough ground with each giant stride.

The click of her camera gained its attention. Monique's adrenaline fuelled legs failed her. All she could do was stare, her wide eyes scarcely able to take in the whole view. Her mouth struggled to form a word. Would it be wow at the wonder of seeing a new species for the first time; or would she scream in terror? Standing to its incredible full height, Monique staggered back, her quick mind already straining to find an escape route

The thud as the dead doe hit the ground was the first sign of the threat. Turning slowly towards her, its deathly dark eyes understood everything. Heart thumping, her mind raced. Should she run? It would catch her. Fighting the urge to flee, she stood no chance. H had plainly earned its trust. Clinging to the possibility it was just curious, she had to stay strong. If she could just stand her ground...

She had met Mari Mathias only a few times, now her mind filled in the gaps in her memory as images of this beast tearing her arms from her body; sinking huge teeth into her pale flesh flooded her thoughts.

Suddenly it charged.

Crashing towards her, its speed removed the option to run. Instinct took over. A gorilla would charge because it was startled. If it could be convinced you were no threat, she knew you were likely to survive with bruises.

But a Chimpanzee would kill you just for the fun of it. And the Bili apes she'd encountered for months in the Congo were the most terrifyingly savage beasts she had ever witnessed. Until now.

The fury in the sasquatch's eyes left her one option. Aiming the puny gun at the monster, now only ten feet away, she screamed at the top of her lungs and jerked the trigger and fired.

The scream, in the desperate charade she wasn't afraid, combined with the pain the beast would suffer, Monique desperately hoped would make it pause and think twice about its unknown foe. It didn't.

Lunging long arms through the air, it threw its huge fist at her head.

"Nooo!" squealed H from in the woods. "Don't."

Her vision blurred from the blow. Crashing to the ground, she wondered if H had meant her or the ape. Pain as another blow from the brute struck her chest fired her survival instinct to pump her with adrenaline. But she'd left it too late to flee.

Hauling her legs up, she desperately covered her face with her hands and lay limp. He had to believe she was dead; maybe then he wouldn't try to kill her.

A prod as strong as an iron bar dug between her ribs and she grunted in pain; just like she wouldn't have done if she *was* dead. The game was up. Huge hands gripped her thighs. She felt a breeze as her back left the moist forest floor, her hair falling in her face as she swung through the air. The sound of a gunshot burst into her ears and she dropped to the ground with immense force.

Double vision failed to focus on the padding feet as they stomped away. Big feet.

Chapter Twenty-eight

The prod she felt to her ribcage now was less harsh, but only just. "I'd be quite justified in shooting you, you know. This is private property."

Monique groaned. She was alive. In pain, but alive.

"You'll need to go to hospital, I suppose." H sighed. "I'll have a look at you first; see if it's worth it. See if you're likely to survive."

"Is it a sasquatch?" she rasped through bleeding lips.

"Oh, come on, Monique, bach. You should be telling me! You're the world-famous primatologist."

"I'd love to study it."

"Oh, I'll bet you would. But that's not going to happen, I'm afraid. And if I don't have your assurance you won't tell anyone—difficult for you, I know—well, I'll have to shoot you."

"You wouldn't!" Monique hissed through the gurgling blood. "You'd never get away with it."

Leaning on his shotgun, he chuckled. "I can get away with a lot of things, Monique Xerri. The only question is, do I want to?"

Monique had no idea what he meant. Performing a quick pat down of her face and torso with stiff fingers, she was relieved that, other than the blood from her mouth and a likely cracked rib, she was okay. It can't have wanted to kill her.

Sitting up, she was able to face her elderly neighbour properly. "So, tell me, H," her beguiling Frenchness hitting its mark, "How long 'ave you been hiding it here?"

"He. Not 'it,' he's a 'he.' And to answer your question: about thirty years." Easing his backside onto a tree stump, he trained his gun on Monique. He needn't have worried; she was no threat. Even at his age, she was too shattered from the attack to move.

"He's locked securely away. You're safe for now." H cleared his throat. "I think he must have washed up on the beach at Wiseman's bridge back in '87, it was. The Atlantic flows uninterrupted here from his North American homeland. A storm set him adrift, I suppose." Staring into the distance, he went on, "Anyway, he headed naturally for the woods which is just opposite the beach. Do you know it?"

Monique nodded. They'd scarcely been to the coast since they'd moved to be near it, but she had walked Jess on the sand once or twice before settling for a drink in the quaint pub there.

"And the path leads from the sea straight to my land, which in turn, if you're a clever sasquatch seeking peace and quiet, steers you to the abandoned mine on top of the hill. None of these houses were here then, of course. He wouldn't have been seen."

"Weren't you scared?"

H chuckled again. "Oh yes. But I'm quite the anthropologist myself, you know. I observed from a distance while it hunted deer and rabbits and hares. He was well-fed and placid. Over time, I gained his trust with gifts and meekness, which now he's under threat, has been invaluable, to be honest," his Welsh lilt made him exhibiting a surreal calm.

Shifting in place, Monique winced from the pain of her ribs.

"You shouldn't have shot him. You can't have hurt him too much, but boy did you piss him off!"

Monique smiled. "I was trying to calculate the risk. In the end I decided he was more chimp than gorilla."

"He's more human. Well not even that, really."

They sat in silence for a few minutes before Monique's curiosity broke the hush.

"So why haven't you shown him to the world. Why keep it to yourself?"

H chuckled again. "Dew, dew, bach. You ask some silly questions." Monique frowned. H's eyes twinkled as he looked at her. "I can't, you silly girl. I'm not allowed!"

"Says who?" Monique was cross now.

"Oh, just about every government you can name. You see, Sasquatch have an 'arrangement.'"

"What sort of arrangement? What do you mean?"

H sighed. How much should he tell her? He'd already told her too much. "Let's just say it would be in no-one's best interest for the public to learn the truth about Bigfoot. Your scientist lot would naturally want to run tests, you know they would. There'd be no stopping them. We can't allow that to happen."

"We?"

H nodded. "I used to consider it *them* and *us,* including myself firmly in '*us*' bracket. But now I understand." H stood and held out his hand. "Do you think you can make it up?"

Monique didn't want to admit how unlikely she feared it might be and offered her hand. H was startlingly strong and hauled her to her feet. Hobbling beside him, arm in arm, they made it to the mine entrance. Closed off with a sophisticated electric gate, it wouldn't look out of place at Fort Knox.

"I have to admit, I expected something cruder."

"I didn't pay for it, Monique. It's a government installation, you see."

Monique didn't, but she hoped she would soon.

The passage beyond was dark. Somewhere deep inside, the grunts of the sasquatch echoed. Fast heavy steps rushed towards them and thudded to a halt a few feet away. Just visible in the brightening dawn, the beast stood back and contemplated her.

His enormity was greater than she'd imagined in her head, and with the ceiling of the mine opening for reference, he appeared even taller and brutish than when he'd charged at her through the trees.

Fighting the urge to rush for a better view, Monique shook her head, "Wow. This is incredible." Raising her camera, it had barely left its perch on her chest when H raised his gun.

"Oh, no, Monique. You must know I can't allow photographs."

Monique nodded and lowered the camera. It went against every instinct, but she knew she had no choice. Moving a tentative step, she gasped and almost fell back to the floor as the huge monster gripped the bars and bared his sharp teeth.

"Now, now, Boris. That's no way to treat a celebrity guest, now is it?" Turning to Monique, H smiled. "He'll forgive you. He knows you were scared and didn't really mean him any harm."

"Okay. But maybe keep the gate closed for a little longer."

H smiled. "That's staying firmly shut. He's not due out again until tonight." Leaning on a rock by the opening, H's face dropped. "It's getting harder, Monique. And poor Mari…"

"Why did he kill her?"

H shrugged. "Wrong place, wrong time." He shifted on the rock, his old bones uncomfortable in the damp morning air. "It's been hard to keep him fed. They've cut down the forest too rapidly; not given time for more trees to grow, and so he's had to stay closer to home, here."

Monique gazed at the old man, a tear in her eye. Why had he protected this big creature for so long? And how were the government involved?

"He's been angry. He used to roam wherever and whenever he wanted, hidden by the foliage of the trees. For months he's had to stay in during the day. The mine's big, but not when you're as big as Boris. I can only let him out to hunt."

"He came back to you, though."

H nodded. "He knows he can't risk being discovered."

"Killing Mari didn't help him with that, did it."

H shook his head. "He's intelligent. Probably more intelligent than us, in his own way. But he has one hell of a temper and he was angry. Angry at his home being destroyed; and at being hungry. Mari Mathias must have met him in the wrong mood."

"There were no traces, I presume; or my husband wouldn't be locked up."

"I know. It's awful, but I had no choice. I couldn't say anything. It was out of my hands. Poor David. They came and cleared up. Threatened me to keep quiet, but the guilt..." His old face fell to his palms, his wrinkled skin sagging in the stretch of his fingers. "It's such a mess, Monique. Such a terrible mess."

The pain was getting worse. A vicious nausea closed her eyes and she fought to open them again. H was turning into a distant haze in front of her. Focussing all her energy to her mind, desperately she listened to his story.

"Thirty years I kept this a secret. I used to work for the MoD; designed miniature one-man tanks amongst other things before retiring back home to Wales. I could have made my fortune. I could have taken pictures and sold them, but I knew I wouldn't be allowed."

"How?" Monique managed to squeeze between her blood-encrusted lips.

"I had access to some top-secret stuff in my role for the Ministry." H shifted from cheek to cheek on his rock. "You must be wondering what's the deal about a big ape?"

Monique nodded.

"Well, you see…" He moved again, mouth opening and closing, no words came until he suddenly blurted, "It's where he comes from. Sasquatches are not from this world, Monique," he paused while it sank in. "That's why it's vital to keep him a secret. Because if he was studied, that would become obvious very quickly."

Monique's mind trembled. Consciousness was fading fast, but she had to stay with it. She had to know what H knew. "And the government can't have those sorts of questions? Why? Wouldn't it be fascinating? People need to know." A new energy rushed through her wrecked body at the indignation.

"It's not our decision. Any doubts I had have been satisfied over the last few weeks since Mari was killed. They've been here." H looked meaningfully into the sky. With a cough he rasped, "Let's just say, I've been warned off."

"By who?"

"By Extra-terrestrials… and the F.B.I."

Monique stifled a laugh. "Oh my god! You've been watching too many films, H," she said.

Ignoring her scepticism, H continued. "Technically, my sasquatch belongs to the United States Government. It's they who have the official agreement."

Monique shook her disbelieving head. "You keep saying this agreement. What are you talking about?"

"The U.S. are the main point of contact. It's why they think they run the show, I suppose. You see, they allow certain TV crews limited access because they recognise the worldwide interest in the Bigfoot legend. But they only give them enough time *not* to find anything." He sighed. "Then scientists can say, 'If there were such a thing as Bigfoot, wouldn't we have found evidence by now, with all these people trying to find him?' in that scathing way they do.

"But the real directive… You won't believe me…" H sighed, deciding to tell anyway. He was relieved of the burden. "It sounds crazy, I know, but the real ones in charge are the ET's! The real directive comes from an alien species far more advanced than we can even conceive. I've seen them, *I* swear to god. I feel an absolute bloody fool saying so, but I think I've gained credibility with what you've already seen, yeah?"

It seemed ludicrous to doubt him, even though he sounded crazy. "They've been here, to these woods," he continued. "They come often, so I've heard. There are sightings all the time from Caldey Island. You know? The island just off Tenby?

Monique nodded.

H took a deep breath. "Yeah. Been coming for years, but I saw them for the first time this week. I'll never forget it"

Monique's eyes struggled to open wide enough to take in what her ears funnelled into her cramping brain. Forcing scepticism aside—she didn't have time for any—eventually she asked. "What do they look like?"

Appreciative for her non-challenge, H perked up. "Like every film; every drawing you've ever seen. Grey skin. Large featureless faces except for those big dark almond eyes." H shuddered. "The eyes... So cold.

"I could understand them. Every word. It was weird, because what I heard was an awful screeching like an injured animal. But in here," he tapped his forehead, "In here I *knew* what they were saying to me, somehow." Trembling, colour leached from his creased old face as he struggled to carry on. "In my mind, I could understand every word. They were concerned their livestock—yes, that's what they called him—had been discovered; a breach of their treaty, they said." H stared deep into Monique's brown eyes. "They're in the middle of an important test to see what effect long term earth-living has on their creatures, you see. In return for their not being exposed, they leave us in peace."

It was too much. Too weird.

From nowhere, a sudden searing light filled the forest; so bright Monique's eyes fluttered to shield her burning retinas. Peering through slits, she watched speechless as a figure walked towards her.

From inside the mine, behind the bars, the sasquatch's grunts and squeals grew deafening.

And then it went black.

Chapter Twenty-nine

Nathan Dale felt naked without his weapon. But the damned airport security failed to recognise his authority despite their countries' diplomatic relations. The mild jolt of panic and the patting of his lumpless jacket was akin to a teenager failing to detect their mobile phone appendage. His phone he could live without, especially when it rang before important meetings. He ripped the vibrating rectangle from his pocket and barked into the microphone, "What!?"

Snorting to express his contempt, he ground his jaw before answering. "You don't need me to tell you what to do... Really? Jeez! Just clear it up and think of a convincing cover story. Why do I have to tell you everything?" He thrust his mobile back in his pocket. Cricking his neck left then right, he was relieved the jeep was slowing down. The sooner he could get that monstrous inconvenience out of the way the better.

Arriving at the town hall, Nathan jumped from the four by four with a gasp, a hand thrust inside his lapel and a pained look flitted on his face. A concerned onlooker might fear cardiac arrest, but of course, it was only the absent firearm.

Anticipating who the trouble makers would be, Nathan visited his captives in the order that suited him. He had no use of the African guide they'd brought into the country. Africans harboured no need for bigfoot legends, what with lion-killing Bili apes in Congo, and every other animal trying to kill you at every turn. So he'd ordered the guide from Democratic Republic of the Congo be returned across the border immediately.

With a half-smile perched on his lips, he considered the next of the prisoners. Jimmy Webb would be a cinch to crack. He knew he'd be grateful for any lifeline Nathan offered.

That left Brad.

Pausing, Nathan shook the hand of the guard outside Brad's room and pushed open the door.

"You'd better have a bloody good explanation why you're keeping me in here, mate," the Aussie yelled at the first sign of Nathan's shape as it filled the doorway. "I had to use the toilet in a flaming bucket for Christ's sake!"

Nathan coughed and offered a weak smile. "Whereas your camp in the Congo had five-star luxury, I presume?"

"It was a bloody sight better than this! Why am I here? I've got all my permits. Your blokes never even asked me for 'em."

Nathan ignored the outburst. He didn't have time to discuss Brad's human rights—or the rights he *thought* he had. "Sit down, Mr Cartwright."

Brad slowly obeyed with a look in his eye portraying it wasn't without controlled consideration. Nathan sat contemplating the man in front of him. Could he *be* more of a cliché? He might as well have corks dangling from his hat. "What do you know about the legend of sasquatch? Bigfoot?"

Brad snorted. "I've never believed it. What do you take me for? There's never been any evidence."

"Despite your own work tracking and photographing recently discovered primates in The Democratic Republic of the Congo? I'm not sure I trust your scepticism. Aren't you even curious?"

"Let me finish. I *didn't* believe in them. But now my esteemed partner, Monique Xerri," he waited for the nod of recognition at the name, "has gone off to photograph them without me. Bitch! She wants the glory for herself."

Nathan nodded. "I've already spoken to Ms Xerri. It's my agreement with her that has led me here to speak with you. You see, Brad, I need your assurances in a very delicate matter."

Brad frowned.

"You have a lot of credibility in the world of anthropology, would you agree?"

"Damned right, mate," Brad grinned.

"If you said there was such thing as a sasquatch, the public would believe you?"

"I'd make flaming sure of it!" Brad cooed before adding, "If they were real."

"That's what I thought." He might not believe now, but Nathan knew he'd soon put two and two together. He'd been close… very close, with Monique. He had to get what he needed now. He took a deep breath. "Which is why I'm going to need you to sign this." Leaning over the table, he passed the document to his captive. Brad read through it, his face reddening with rage as he did.

"No way! Who the fuck *are* you, mate? I'm not signing a damned thing. If I can prove a fucking bigfoot is real, I'll go down in history. Why would I give that up?"

"Nathan Dale, FBI, to answer your first question. And, because things will get very difficult for you if I don't get your full compliance, to answer your second." He let his face cloud in the menacing way he practised in the mirror. Brad didn't flinch.

"Well, Mr Nathan Dale, FBI. You don't have any jurisdiction over me. I'm an Australian citizen. Why don't you go back to Yanky-land and take your stupid bit of paper with you?"

A vein in Nathan's neck bulged at the audacity. Being in the FBI had given him power. And since his sasquatch specialisation, he'd basically had licence to do whatever the fuck he wanted to keep the legend under control. Anyone who knew the truth understood who was really running the show. And as long as our cousins from beyond the cosmos wanted sasquatch out of the public domain, they weren't about to be satisfied by issues in U.S./Aussie international relations!

"Either you sign the non-disclosure agreement, or you'll never leave this room!" Nathan slammed his fist on the table but still Brad didn't flinch.

Face clouding in contemplation, he fixed Nathan's gaze. He'd rather his parched eyes fell out and crunched on the floor than succumb to his raging impulse to blink. Once certain his dominance had been imposed, Brad spoke in a measured calm. "Alright, sport. Don't get your knickers in a twist. I didn't realise it was so flaming important. Apologies," he raised his palms. "Don't sweat. I'll sign your bloody paper."

His rapid turnaround was unconvincing. Brad had been right about Nathan's limited power. The agreement he was insisting upon was scarcely worth the paper it was written on—legally. He could appeal. He could go to the press. And something in the twinkle in Brad's eyes as he scribbled his name told Nathan all he needed to know.

"Thank you. That wasn't so hard, was it now?" Nathan smirked with satisfaction. Standing, he examined the freshly signed document and smiled. "I knew you'd come around. I'll go and make the arrangements."

Brad grinned from his perfect tan. "No worries."

Nathan hauled open the door. Before walking out, he turned and smiled again at Brad. "Goodbye, Mr Cartwright," he said with a nod.

Within two steps down the corridor, his face clouded like a tropical storm. Shaking his head in quick jerks, Nathan raised a thick finger to his throat. He motioned its slicing with a sickening glare.

The man in the beret, clutching the machine gun with the natural ease a smoker proffers a cigarette, barked his order to the guards at the door. "Kui," he said with the same throat-slitting motion. "Kill."

Chapter Thirty

Jimmy regarded the door opening with the same absence he'd adhered to throughout his sleepless night. A bucket, and a tray of bread and water had been brought at some point. In a daze, he had profited from all three.

And now they were gone, replaced by a figure in the doorway. As the tall, broad man blocked the light from the hallway, stood silhouetted, hand outstretched, Jimmy's eyes narrowed and he gasped. As the light hit the side of his face, Jimmy was sure: the lawyer from Swansea prison. What was he doing here?

"Mr Webb," he addressed, removing, without a care, the offer of a handshake when Jimmy's paralysis prevented it being seized. He squeezed himself into the chair on the other side of the rickety table. Barely fit for the job of supporting his granite bulk, it creaked in distress as Nathan placed his huge hands flat in front of him. "Listen carefully."

Jimmy's brain jolted. This was going to be important. A lawyer from U.K. originating from U.S.A. was here, in an African prison with him. This had to represent hope. Jimmy listened.

"What do you know about sasquatch?"

Jimmy frowned. When he tried to speak, his voice croaked. "What do you mean?"

Nathan sighed. "This is gonna take forever if you can't answer a simple fucking question. What I mean is what I say. Answer me in plain English and you never know, you might make it out of here alive."

Jimmy sat up. "Aren't you my lawyer? Aren't you here to get me out of this place?"

Nathan stared. "No, Jimmy. I'm not your fucking lawyer. I'm the one who dragged your sorry ass out of the jungle. That's who I am."

Jimmy gulped. What was going on? He decided he would do his best to obey the simple instructions. "I know my brother thinks he saw one near his house, and that he thinks it killed our neighbour, Mari Mathias. I know they're big and fast and elusive and no-one really believes in them."

"And yet you decided to contact a well-known American TV show to come all the way to fucking Wales because 'no-one believes in them?'"

Nathan still stared, so Jimmy babbled on, unsure if believing or not-believing was the way out of this. "They didn't find anything… One of the local kids thinks they kill cows and eat their lips." That still sounded ridiculous. "Er, that's about it."

"*They kill cows and eat their lips*," Nathan scribbled notes. "You believe in them, Jim, yeah? Is that fair to say?"

After a second where his brain offered alternatives to the truth, Jimmy opted for "Yeah." He didn't understand enough to lie his way out of this.

Nathan nodded and offered his attempt at a warm smile. "I'm with the FBI. This," he gestured generally around, "is a matter of international importance. So, before we go any further, I'm going to need you to sign these." He shoved a wad of papers across the table, followed by a pen. Jimmy began reading, his eyes widening with every word.

"So they are real! Bigfoot is real. Oh my god. I knew it."

"Just sign the papers, Jim."

Jimmy scribbled his moniker where Nathan pointed with his broad finger.

"Good. Well done." Nathan smiled and leaned across the table. Then, with a sudden rush of movement, he grabbed Jimmy's collar and brought his face hurtling towards the table.

As the wind rushed past, he cried out, "Hey!" before his lips smacked into the wood rendering him mute.

"I don't know if this is going to be enough, Jimmy. You get me, Jim? I'm not convinced your signed agreement is worth a goddam thing."

"Hmmm mmmph," is all Jimmy could muster.

"You're a mess. A drunk, drugged-up, fucking mess. Who knows what you'll do; or what you'll say to get your next fix?" Assured he had his captive's full attention, Nathan released his grip and threw him back in his chair.

Jimmy rasped for air, timid tears streaking his grubby cheeks. "I won't say anything! I won't tell anyone. I'd feel stupid anyway," he squealed.

"Oh, you might not mean to, Jimmy. But if you could sell your story, you could buy a lot of Heroin, couldn't you?" Nathan spat.

"I'm off that now. Haven't touched it in ages."

"But you're never really off it. Not completely. And you're a drunk. Drunks aren't so hot at keeping secrets."

"I will. I promise."

"Again, Jimmy; what's your promise worth?"

Jimmy sagged forward and palmed his face. He was right. What was his promise worth? How many times had he sworn to his mum, dad and brother that he was clean?

How many times had they bailed him out? "I don't know," he whimpered.

Nathan Dale stood. "At least you're being honest. I appreciate honesty. Here's the thing…" Pacing the room one more time, he spun his chair round and straddled it like a little orange plastic pony. "There's no way I can let this get out; I mean about bigfoot marauding round West Wales. It can't happen. Do you understand?"

Jimmy raised his face and met Nathan square in the eye to assure him of his trustworthiness, but he couldn't hold his gaze.

"It's not that it would be a pain," Nathan drawled, "it would be absolutely catastrophic. I can't explain more." Jimmy shook his head. He was surprised, he didn't want to know. Ignorance was bliss. "Suffice it to say, I'm deadly serious. D.e.a.d.l.y."

Turning his gaze up to kill, Nathan deepened his voice. "If I think there's a chance; the slightest *hint* I can't trust you, then I can't let you leave this room." He sighed. "It would be so easy. Plenty of people don't return from this part of the world. If the civil unrest doesn't catch up with you, a lion or a fucking ape probably will. And that's not counting hundreds of goddam insects and snakes all tryin' to kill you. Oh, you never leaving here would be the easiest thing in the world. Believe me."

Jimmy did believe him. Jimmy totally believed him.

Standing, Nathan walked to the window. Glancing back into the room and to his prisoner, Nathan relaxed his tone. "Listen, Jimmy, I like you. You're a fuck up, but you're an honest fuck up. I'll tell you now: I may have a use for you. Maybe I'll hold off on killing you until I know how this is gonna pan out. Call it a reprieve, if you will. You never know, Jimmy. Maybe this can be a new start. A new 'James Webb.'" Nathan lowered the threat with the ease of changing a snapchat filter. "Here's what I'm going to do." He took a deep breath. "I'm going to give you a chance…"

Jimmy gasped. The tear of gratitude in his eye blurred his vision. Could this actually turn out to be what he needed? "Oh, thank you," he burbled. "You won't regret it."

Switching the switch, Nathan growled, "Make sure I don't." Leaning across the table again, allowing his face to fall into the grotesque and terrifying snarl he relied on so much, Nathan refrained from a physical attack this time. He didn't want a mess on the floor. "If ever you're tempted to brag to any of your stupid, drunk, druggie little chums for whatever reason… Don't!"

Jimmy shook his head in quick rapid jerks.

Shifting his snarling lips still closer, Nathan growled, "I'll be watching. I'll be listening… Every phone call; every conversation; every time you log onto the World Wide Web, I'll be there." A string of angry saliva fell from Nathan's white teeth onto Jimmy's hand. Jimmy made no move to wipe it. The bulging eyes before him had his full attention.

"If I get so much as a sniff you've been indiscreet, there will be no second chances. You'll be discovered in some back alley with a needle sticking out of your arm, pumped up to your eyeballs with a lethal hit of Heroin. You'll die the shameful disgusting death you deserve!"

Nathan stood up and beamed. "Or, you can keep your mouth shut and make something of yourself. What do you say?"

This time, Jimmy took the hand in his own trembling grip. "That one."

Nathan rolled his hand in the air for Jimmy to elaborate.

"I'll keep quiet and make something of myself."

Nearly crushing Jimmy's hand in his incredible grip, Nathan slapped him on the arm, "Attaboy!" he beamed. A confirmatory nod prompted Jimmy to rise from his seat and follow. Outside, a car waited and they hopped inside.

"Why did you come here, to Africa?" Jimmy asked. "Why not just get me on the plane, or at the airport?"

Nathan grinned. "I like to move immediately. I knew this way, you'd understand I'd find you anywhere if I came out here. I wanted you to be in no doubt what I'm capable of."

Jimmy slowly nodded. There could be no question. The terror he'd faced here was much more persuasive than anything else he could imagine. He supposed what he'd really meant was how was he even worth it? Was he really that much of a threat to national and international security? Li'l-ol-Jimmy Webb? The notoriety carved a grin on his exhausted face. Wow.

As if reading his mind, Nathan added, "And, of course, it wasn't just you I had to silence, was it…" he let the words hang, but Jimmy didn't get the message.

They'd driven half-an-hour towards the airport when Jimmy's eyes clouded with confusion as the alluded threat burnt into his cloggy mind. "What about Brad?" he blurted. "Isn't he coming with us?"

Nathan's face clouded and he shook his head. "Add Brad to the list of stuff I don't want you to talk about," he growled. Staring through his sunglasses out of the window, it was clear the subject was closed.

With a gulp of dire realisation at Brad's fate, Jimmy mumbled, "Okay," and sank back in his seat in silence.

Chapter Thirty-one

A booming greeting filled the silence, "How are you feeling?" Monique didn't recognise the voice. Wincing, she opened her eyes slowly. Touching her ribs, she nodded, mouth turned down at the lack of pain. This was good. "We have a problem." The owner of the voice let out a little cough. "Or rather *you* have a problem."

Monique sat upright now. She was surprised to be in her own lounge, on her own sofa. "Who are you?" she demanded, her voice startling her with its potency, her lips incredibly repaired.

"Nathan Dale," a large man in a sharp suit stepped forward and plucked gold-rimmed sunglasses from his chiselled face. "I'm with the FBI."

It was like being plonked in a film.

"How much do you recall of last night?"

Last night? She really had healed quickly. The huge sasquatch; the long talk with H; that was crystal clear. But then a hazy image of something... she wasn't sure. She shuddered.

Nathan shifted his weight to his other foot and gregariously opened his shoulders in a show of supreme confidence. "I don't know if I can trust you, Monique, so I'm just gonna go on ahead and assume you remember the whole damned thing. Which is where this issue of a problem arises."

He rested his large square frame on the arm of the sofa; far too close for politeness. She could see the holster of his gun under his jacket. She didn't think he'd need it.

"You are in the unfortunate position of knowing too much, Monique Michelle Xerri." She got the feeling he used her full name so she was in no doubt his research was thorough. "And if we can't trust you, we have to come up with a plan."

Drumming his hand on his raised thigh, he swung round and stood. Before speaking, he paced the room, then stopped abruptly, making sure Monique witnessed the smile leave his face. In its place was a coldness she'd never before seen. And that was after years of studying savage wild animals. She knew he was deadly serious.

"Here's my plan: I can make it so you never got on that plane; so that you never left Africa. It's volatile right now... Who am I kidding? It's always volatile, right?" The big American white-toothed smile returned for a split second, then disappeared. He was in complete control.

"I'd leave you in Africa, doing your thing with the Bili apes and Brad. Oh yeah. We know everything," he answered Monique's raised eyebrow. "But you might meet an unfortunate end. Maybe you won't come back when you're expected; you, Brad, and your dopey brother-in-law."

"Jimmy?" Monique gasped.

"Didn't you know?" he said, knowing she didn't. "He came to find you. He musta reckoned you'd be just the one to prove our little secret to the public. And, unfortunately for us all, he was right."

Leaning over her from his robust height, Nathan sneered. "Everyone will assume you've been taken by a guerrilla group. Lord knows there's enough of them; we'll arrange contact from them: something for the press to get their teeth into." He laughed. "And then, when we're sure any correlation between your husband's ridiculous allegations of a bigfoot in Pembrokeshire has been forgotten," he let his eyes cross at the absurdness of it, "Then we'll break the news you've all been found dead."

He clapped his hands making Monique jump. "That's my plan, and to be frank, I think it's the best one we have."

Colour drained from Monique's tanned face. She would treat this monster like any she'd dealt with in the wild: remain calm and stand her ground. "What if I refuse to go back to Africa?"

Nathan shook his head. His lips parted into a genuine laugh. "You wouldn't *actually* go back to the Congo." Frowning, he chuckled, "Did you really think that? Wow. I thought I was being unambiguous."

He paced some more before standing facing her, hands on hips; the stance leaving his jacket open and his holster exposed.

"You've seen *Men in Black,* yeah? You must have," he nodded along to his own hypothesis. "Well, you know the bit when they use the little flashy things that make you forget? That'd be great right now, wouldn't it?"

Monique didn't know what to say.

"Well, I do kind of have one of those," he grinned; then, in a rapid jerk, he thrust his hand into his jacket and un-holstered his pistol. Swiping the gun to her forehead in one well-rehearsed motion, he forced the muzzle into her skin. Monique flinched, smarting from the sting of the hard tip digging into her head.

Eyes bulging, Monique knew she couldn't let her terror show. Desperate to control the shaking she felt in her legs, she stared at the grimacing face; mouth snarling, teeth bared, a dribble of saliva spun from his top lip to his bottom lip like a spider's snare. His finger extended to the trigger, and from the stretched tendon in his hand, he was itching to pull it. Monique closed her eyes. "This works real well!" he spat. "I pull the trigger, and you don't remember a goddam thing!"

With considerable effort, Nathan forced the gun away from Monique's skull and re-holstered it. He'd made his point. "I guess it would be sad. Your children shouldn't grow up without their mum. That's to say; you'd be here even less than you are now." The remark stung more than the muzzle of the pistol. It was true. She spent so much time away on photo-shoots, she felt like a guest in her own home.

"Long-suffering David, bless him. He'd have to stay in prison. Of course, he'd find out about you and his brother dying out in Africa. I don't imagine he'd take it well: who knows, he may never make it home. I suppose I can see some sense in at least trying to think of another plan."

He sighed and sat beside her. Giving her thigh a gentle pat, he was doing a great job of good-cop, bad-cop all by himself. He was crazy. "My superiors; and you better believe I mean it: you don't want to mess with these guys. You met them last night."

Monique gasped. "Met..?" she mumbled.

Nathan ignored her and carried on. "Well, they have a different plan." Removing his hand from her thigh, he brought it to meet his other resting between his knees. He'd gone from psychopath to lost little boy in seconds.

"My agency only became aware of a non-American sasquatch weeks ago. A short while after your husband. Since then we installed caging to keep him, and the public, safe. But our friends from above, they've known all along. They've been visiting and experimenting, as they love to do, for decades."

Monique could see the sweat beading on Nathan's brow. "But as soon as there's a problem, we're blamed for violating our agreement to keep them secret. Man!" he sighed. "They don't help themselves. Killing cows, taking weird shit. I don't even have a clue what they do with the lips, for Christ's sake. And why do they have to dump them so conspicuously?" he sighed. "*We* have to clear up their mess. Surely they could be more discreet?" He shook his head.

"It's like they want us to mess up… like they're looking for an excuse…" He left the phrase hanging in the air. Monique had no idea what to say. "Anyway," he regained his composure enough to include more of his usual bluster as he said, "They seem to like you. And they think you can help them."

Monique fell back in her seat. First, an old man, now this international agent, both telling her about *them.* She still didn't believe who *they* were, but hearing she'd had contact… She shuddered recalling the shadowy figure approaching from the blistering light in the woods.

"H is old," Nathan continued. "He can't do what he's been doing for much longer. We can't be sure he's up to it, can we? I mean, come on! He looks about a hundred. I wanted to take our Bigfoot back to The States, but *they* want the Welsh data… go figure."

Nathan smiled again, and this time it was real. "Don't look so down. This could be good. If you agree, everything can work out. And you get to know stuff no-one else does! It's a primatologist's dream!"

Monique cocked her head. She couldn't wait to hear how this might actually be beneficial.

"You'd have to gain its trust. H can help with the transition to your care. You will report to us, let it out to hunt, and make sure it comes back in without doing any harm." Nathan peered down at her, a chilling glint in his eye. "We won't risk another incident."

Seeing Monique's uneasiness, he repeated, "H will show you. Basically, if it's extra hungry, lead it to food. Study it. You can do that, can't you Monique? It's just up your street, I should think."

As the incredible offer sank in, excitement bubbled deep within Monique. The opportunity to top a lifetime's passion lay before her: to study a creature, legendary in its notoriety. It was a dream come true, surely.

"David would be free," Nathan went on, "Jimmy could be allowed back. Marcus and Sara would be safe home with their mum and their dad." Hitting his broad chest with a square fist, he said in an upbeat tone. "And I could go home, happy this little problem was being taken care of."

"And if I refuse?"

Nathan's face clouded again. "I don't know why they like you, Monique! I thought I'd made it very clear. Listen! This goes beyond trust. You'll have to sign your fucking life away... literally. You understand?"

Monique nodded quickly.

"You sure? Cos you don't seem so smart, to me."

"I understand. Sorry."

Nathan relaxed again. "Good."

At risk of another tirade, Monique plastered on her most alluring smile before asking, "I won't be able to pursue my usual career," she cooed. "I mean," slender tanned fingers rested on her neck, "I'll need to stay here, won't I?"

Nathan nodded.

"Well, how will we manage? I do make a fair bit."

"Oh my god! You're asking for money!"

Flinching, Monique cringed awaiting her captor's anger. Instead, he grinned and let out a raucous guffaw. "Now you're talking my language! Don't worry, you'll be looked after."

There was an uncomfortable silence before Nathan jolted as if he'd just remembered something. Walking into the hallway, he pulled on the front door and beckoned to the driver of a big black car parked in the driveway. He watched as the back door opened and a figure appeared from behind the tinted glass.

Flanked by two men dressed similarly to Nathan, the figure was led carefully inside. A wry smile played on Nathan's mouth at the head trembling beneath the bag covering it. Gesturing towards the lounge, the figure was shuffled along by the two men until they stood before Monique.

Gazing with bulging eyes set to fall from their sockets, she hissed, "What is thiss? What is going on?"

The head beneath the sack cloth made some incomprehensible noises. Nathan guided Monique's quivering fingers to the cloth hood and forced it into her grasp. With a nod, he cajoled her to remove it. What would she see?

The material flapped in her weak grip. Gritting her teeth, she flung the hood back and flinched away. Tears of joy burning her cheeks, she recognised who was beneath. Leaping up she threw her arms around her brother-in-law and kissed his snivelling face. "Jimmy. Oh Jimmy, you are safe. I am so happy!"

Tears flooded from them as they held one another in unprecedented warmth. Nathan Dale squeezed both their shoulders as he shook with mirth. Monique glared at him, but Jimmy just clung onto Monique, hopeful this was all over.

"Excuse my sense of humour. I couldn't resist." His eyes darkening, he leaned in for a final word. "I'm going now. My colleagues here will put things in place with H. Don't let me down, and remember, if I'm forced to come back to this shitty little island because you're not up to the job, I'm going to be real pissed! And I am one sadistic bastard."

Releasing his grip, he walked back to the front door. Turning before stepping outside, he called out to Monique and Jimmy. "You all have a real nice day now, you hear?" and he was gone.

Collapsing on the sofa, the pair clutched onto one-another. Grasping Jimmy's hand, fearful to ask, Monique mouthed to her brother-in-law; 'Brad?'

Jimmy shook his head in rapid jerks. His wide eyes shone with horror.

No words were spoken.

None were needed.

Chapter Thirty-two

"**D**avid Webb? You have a visitor."

David sighed. Hauling himself from the bench, he dreaded who it could be. And when he saw the hulking threat that was Nathan Dale, he almost turned and went back to his cell.

"What do you want?" he sneered.

"David, old buddy, old pal. I've got great news."

"What?"

"You're free to go."

David staggered backwards, knocking his chair over. He expected a prison guard to run over at the commotion, but no-one came. Pulling the chair from the floor and righting it, he sat down on the edge and perched his arms on the table. "Why? How? I haven't been to trial."

Nathan shrugged. "There won't be a trial. What can I say? They made a mistake. Not enough evidence after all."

"How?" David's wispy voice queried again.

"Look. Don't be a big Dumbo, Dave. Can I call you Dave?" David didn't care. "We know what happened, don't we? We know the truth. We just had to bend it there for a while until we could figure out what to do."

"Do?" David's clumsy lips dropped into the room without expectation of an answer, but what he heard next brought reality quickly into focus.

"Sorry, friend. I realise you haven't had the best time. Oh, and there's stuff you might be wondering about, well I'm sure you must be. The DNA in Mari's car? That was us." Nathan smiled. "Her incriminating diary? Us too. We made it up, I'm afraid. There was no DNA. There was no diary." He put his hands up, palms out, crinkling his lips. "My bad."

Clasping his face in clammy fingers, David's incredulous mouth mumbled, "What's changed?"

Nathan leaned back on his plastic chair, straining its integrity to almost breaking. "Let's just say that thanks to your neighbour, H, and your lovely wife, we've come to an arrangement whereby it's no longer necessary to keep you locked up."

David's mind whirled. "H? Monique? What do you mean?"

"They know about what you saw, Dave. H has been keeping it secret for years. Now it's your turn." Leaning in, he lowered his voice. "There'll be paperwork for you to sign, you know?"

"What paperwork?" David whimpered.

Lunging across the table, grabbing David by the collar, Nathan drew him close. The coffee on his breath combined with a minty fresh oddness as he spat his words. "Oh, just that if you ever breathe a word of this to

226

a living soul, I'll kill you and every single one of your fucking family!" he threw David back in his seat and leaned back again. "That's all."

Pushing himself back from the table, he stood and grinned as he thrust out his huge hand. "What do you say?"

In a daze, David watched detached as his own limp specimen raised in the air. Nathan grabbed it and they shook hands.

The deal was done.

Chapter Thirty-three

Two months later...

"Will you come with me to feed Boris today?"

David gulped. Every time he even thought about the beast in H's field, images of it charging down the valley towards him, and then of what it did to poor Mari screamed in his mind.

"Or shall I get the children to do it?" Minique smiled. Her accountant husband, so solid and safe; she had to be careful what she asked of him. She had faced off with dangerous animals for decades. The closest he came to danger was the end of the tax year. "I'll make sure to be back in time," she grinned. The dropping of tension from David's shoulders made her eyes twinkle. Throwing her long tanned legs from the bed, she declared, "I'm going to shower."

"Wait. I wanted to ask... I thought we could visit Mari's grave. Maybe at the weekend... Shame we missed her funeral."

Monique squeezed his arm. It was all over for them. Mari's death could be considered a terrible accident. But knowing Boris now; being responsible for him, gave them a sense of guilt it was difficult to appease. "Why not," she cooed as she raised herself from the bed.

David watched his beautiful wife disappear, rolled contentedly onto his back and stared at the ceiling. It had been a remarkable year. Whatever had happened in Congo had been a blessing for their marriage. Monique never even mentioned Brad.

Because she didn't gallivant around the world anymore, David supposed she had no need of her intrepid, ruggedly handsome guide. But he would have expected her to shoehorn him in sometimes. He chuckled. All this time worrying about the two of them, and it had only ever been work—just as she'd always insisted. Anything between them had been in the distant past before they'd even met. And she had chosen him. The gaping grin threatened to turn his face inside-out. She loved him, her ever-faithful (after-all) husband. That was clear.

When Nathan Dale's arrangements had been outlined to him, he feared his wife would be restless. But her new work caring for and studying Bigfoot Boris satisfied her immensely; the sasquatch was more of a threat to win her affection than Brad had ever been, he chuckled to himself.

And she had readers of her reports too. Every week she would send her findings to high up government scientists from here and across the pond. Her readership was small but very appreciative.

And there was enough money in the pot for them to demonstrate their gratitude handsomely. In all measurable ways, they were better off: They never wanted for anything; they saw one-another every day (and without David being worried); his children had a newfound respect for the father who had been prepared to rot in jail to save his family; and even Jimmy had a job. Just a start, at a local 'Family farm' open to the public with a petting zoo and fairground rides. And he was clean.

As the water washed over her, Monique smiled a contented smile. Her life was so fascinating now. One day, she imagined, Sara and Marcus might take over her life's work. Nobody was sure how long a sasquatch lived for. She was already so attached to the big brute that she dreaded the day she might find out.

It was possible he could live for hundreds of years. The only ones who might know: the ones who brought him here, weren't about to say. That's if they even knew themselves.

Shaking her head in disbelief, the thought passed that she was actually insane; that she had imagined everything, and when she stepped from the shower she would find a nurse ready to take her back to her padded cell amongst all the others who believed in Bigfoot and little green men.

The laughter built in her stomach and expanded her chest, then exploded in hysterical guffaws. She wasn't surprised when David rushed in to see if she was okay. Opening the shower door, she smiled her gap-toothed grin. "I'm fine. More than fine... Care to join me? You can scrub my back."

She let her alluring bent-over pose slide as she watched her husband fumbling with the drawstring of his paisley pyjamas. What a sex-god, she giggled, before he was finally free and joining her in the steam.

"Come here you sexy swine," she soothed. Flicking playfully between his legs, she kissed him. "What is this? Is it the *Beast of* Benfro? David laughed. How could he ever have doubted the love of his wonderful wife?

Epilogue

Judy sat and rocked in her chair. A bird flying into the window made her heart stop, and then race to catch up on precious moments lost.

Guilt sucked the colour from her face as she remembered. If only she'd called out, he might have made it back to the house. Instead, she had watched in silent disbelief as her husband had suffered his third and final cardiac arrest, and then did nothing but stare as the awful creature dragged him away.

She had told no-one. Who *could* she tell? And now, months later, people were beginning to ask questions. Understandable, justifiable questions like: "Where's Dad?"

She'd held it together, but even from eleven thousand miles away in Tasmania their daughter had known something was amiss.

Rocking harder and faster, Judy didn't know what to say. If Beau's disappearance was discovered, her life would be over too. There was blood. Lots of blood. The police would ask questions and come to the wrong conclusions, and who could blame them?

She'd certainly done nothing to disguise it; to wash it away. She hadn't left the house. Instead, not by choice, she had left the carrion for rain and flies to do their thing, and the guilt twisted and wounded like a rusty sabre.

Peeping from her window when the Tesco driver arrived with her measly order, she flinched at each movement from the trees convinced the beast might jump and devour him at any moment.

But she couldn't leave. She couldn't even go outside.

Judy knew she could never leave her home again.

And, of course, Judy wasn't the only captive in the hills and valleys of Pembrokeshire. High up on the peak, the sasquatch peered out between the bars. Gripping them hard, his hairy knuckles whitened and he turned away. There was no budging them, but he had a plan.

The mine shaft was long. Most of it had caved in long ago, but he'd been moving rocks. When, he wasn't sure, but one day he would remove the final stone and step outside through another entrance on another hill.

He would have to stay hidden, he knew. *Them* coming back for him was to be avoided at all costs. He never wanted to see them again. Breathing hard, he pounded his frustration on the rock wall sending echoes through the tunnels. Patience. That's all he needed.

Hungry, he paused before beginning his work again for a snack. Bending, he picked up a fleshy bone from his cold store. Picking cloth from between his teeth, he bit down hard to the crunch.

Eyes falling on his latest kill, he squinted. Regret wasn't an emotion he recognised, but it was with something approaching remorse that he surveyed the mighty panther hanging from the strut holding up the ceiling. That would last him a few days. By then he may be free again.

In a wild flurry, he beat his chest and flung what was left of Beau's stripped leg into the depths of darkness. Seething, he fumbled his mighty hand around on the floor. Finding what he was looking for, he clutched the bearded face close to his own and stared at the bony sockets where lifeless eyes had shrivelled.

With a snarl of contempt, he hurled Beau's skull at the wall, the crack and thud as it rolled on the floor soothed him. Rummaging through remains on the cavern floor, he grunted that his hand failed to fall on the other, fresher skull. Clenching his fist, he thumped the ground. The blood of his foolish enemies would soon run if he was denied his freedom for much longer, he promised himself.

Snorting through huge flat nostrils, he calmed his breathing, reached down and moved one of the rocks. Behind it sat another, then another, and another. But he knew; he sensed, there would come a break and he would shift the final barrier between captivity and freedom.

And he had all the time in the world...

Report from the Tenby Herald:

Pembrokeshire Mental health services came under fire this week, criticised over their handling of local farmer, Glyn Evan's, suicide. Sources tell us he was not even on their radar.

The husband of Susan Evans ne Lewis took a shotgun into his field where he had erected a small tent, inside which he used the gun to take his own life.

The service has been condemned for not offering better support for the distress he had suffered at the death of two out of area 'wild campers', Graham and Karen Hatton of Hertfordshire, who were trampled to death by cattle on Mr Evan's farm.

His shocked and devastated wife, Susan, said he had kept the whole incident from her and went on to add, '*He shouldn't have felt guilty at all. It's not permitted to camp on our land and tourists should always use the official sites. There are no shortage of them, and now because of their selfishness, I'm left without my husband.*'

Our sympathies are with the families of all the deceased at this sad time.

I hope you enjoyed this book. If you have, perhaps I can ask you the favour of telling your friends about it?

As an independent author I don't have the support of a large publishing house with their budget for promotions, and so I rely heavily on word-of-mouth recommendations.

Another easy way to help that makes the world of difference is to post a review; just a line or two reassuring potential readers they should take a chance on my books.

If you are able to help, here's a link to the Amazon page

If you would like to read more, the following pages are for you...

A sneak preview snippet from the sequel to *The Beast of Benfro,* entitled **_The Hunt For The Beast of Benfro_**

Enjoy...

Zipping up his warm coat despite the mildness of the evening, he wasn't sure how long it would take.

As he strolled past the few houses on his way to H's field, he wondered if any of them had the faintest idea of the dangerous monster that lived only a few hundred metres from their house. Most of them were elderly and didn't venture too far into the wilderness, saving their energy for walks to the shop, but the old Victorian school had been converted into homes occupied by far younger residents. Was his family's job to warn the children not to play on the field because of the abandoned mine shafts like H had done to him, or was the old man still up to the task? It was his land after all. He'd ask Monique later.

With one foot two rungs up the gate, David swung his leg around and hopped to the ground. Just knowing he was sharing a field with the beast who he'd first seen hurtling down the hillside a few weeks ago sent a shudder down his spine.

Heading for the trees, he hated the next part of the night's job: preparing the food. At least it was safe.

With every stride his heart sank. He knew he had no choice but the reality of his gruesome chore stuck in his throat, threatening to exit explosively. Pausing to swallow, he closed his eyes. Pushed on by the degrading opinions his wife and children had of his capabilities he took another step forward, then another, and another and he arrived; at the barn.

Through the door, he could hear the hooves clopping. Did they never rest or did they somehow sense his approach and what he was about to do?

Keying in the code on the lock, the bolts slid allowing David access to the central stalls. The herd beyond, behind the bars, edged back. They knew. He was sure they knew.

How could he choose one? How could he choose which would die tonight? They would all meet the same fate in the end, so did it even matter? There were no weak ones; no stragglers he could pick off. Unhooking the harness and lead from its place by the gate, he slid the bolt aside and pushed.

The mighty beasts cowered in his presence. He had been here before with Monique, but he found it strange they recognised him. Was he giving off a scent? The stench of death?

"Come on, fella. I'm afraid it's your turn." The nearest deer growled and put down its head and slunk backwards. What would he do if it resisted? How did his wife cope? Pulling out some pony nuts from his pocket, he offered out a flat hand. A different deer, more a fawn really, offered tentative lips to David's palm and snuffled the treats from his hand. Grabbing fresh supply from his pocket he re-offered them to the young deer.

Confident this time, the animal relaxed. Even as David slipped the collar around its neck it carried on eating. Pressed against the back wall, its family looked distraught but resigned. A creature so trusting of its enemy was never going to be a good addition to the gene pool. Not that many of these creatures would get to contribute in that regard.

Clipping the carabiner onto the collar, he made a clicking noise with his tongue on the inside of his cheek, the one reserved for hooved animals in the same way *'puss puss,'* was used for cats, and the adolescent trailed willingly behind.

As he closed the gate, leaving just him and the chosen animal in the entrance stall, he wondered what it would think. Might it wonder if it had been selected to have freedom in the forest. Would it miss its family or relish the liberty? How long before it realised its true purpose? David prayed not until the last moment, but he feared he was being a fool. If they dreaded his presence, he could only imagine how they suffered smelling Boris.

Monique always let the chosen animal free because Boris enjoyed the hunt. But David felt reluctant. He knew what would happen if he wasn't fed and there was a lot of forest for a little creature to hide in. What if the locks didn't work and delayed letting him out? What if he momentarily forgot the code? He couldn't risk the sasquatch killing another unsuspecting Pleasant Valley resident, so, with great reluctance, he paused at a tree, far enough away from the barn, but close enough for Boris to have an easy find.

Looping the rein around the tree, he tied it securely. Reaching his hand into his pocket for the remaining snacks, he fed them to the little deer. "I'm sorry, so so sorry. You're making a valiant sacrifice, fella. It's complicated, but believe me when I tell you I have no choice."

As he walked away, fear hit the fawn as it tugged against the lead. The tree held firm and it knew it was trapped. David was sure it sensed why.

He couldn't look back. Batting snotty tears from his face, he forced himself forward. If that was hard, how would he struggle to release its killer into the woods?

Because he had no choice. That's how.

I hope you enjoyed this excerpt. To order this novel, use this link:

http://viewbook.at/Hunt-for-the-Beast

And for more of Michael's books, follow this link to your local Amazon:

http://author.to/MCCarter

Join Michael's reader group for updates on latest releases and get a free ebook

https://www.michaelchristophercarter.co.uk/no-1-hot-new-release-free

About the author

Michael grew up in the leafy suburbs of Hertfordshire in the eighties. His earliest school memories from his first parent's evening were being told "You have to be a writer"; advice Michael didn't take for another thirty-five years, despite a burning desire.

Instead, he forged a career in direct sales, travelling the length and breadth of Southern England selling fitted kitchens, bedrooms, double-glazing and conservatories, before running his own water-filter business (with an army of over four hundred water filter salesmen and women) and then a conservatory sales and building company.

All that came to an end when Michael became a carer for a family member and moved to Wales, where he finally found the time and inspiration to write.

Michael now indulges his passion in the beautiful Pembrokeshire Coast National Park where he lives, walks and works with his wife, four children and Golden Retriever.

Made in the USA
Coppell, TX
22 October 2022